Miranda
Goes to
Hollywood

ALSO BY JANE KENDALL

Miranda and the Movies

JANE KENDALL

Miranda Goes to Hollywood

Adventures in the Land of Palm Trees, Cowboys, and Moving Pictures

HARCOURT BRACE & COMPANY

San Diego   New York   London

For Luisa

Library of Congress Cataloging-in-Publication Data
Kendall, Jane F.
Miranda goes to Hollywood: adventures in the land of palm trees,
cowboys, and moving pictures/by Jane Kendall.
p.   cm.
Companion title to: Miranda and the movies.
Summary: In 1915, having been introduced to the exciting
world of making movies the previous summer, twelve-year-old
Miranda follows The American Moving Picture Company
to Hollywood to embark on a film career.
ISBN 0-15-202059-4
[1. Motion pictures—Production and direction—Fiction.
2. Hollywood (Los Angeles, Calif.)—Fiction.
3. Actors and actresses—Fiction.]   I. Title.
PZ7.K334Mj   1999
[Fic]—dc21   98-30912

Text set in Goudy
Designed by Linda Lockowitz

First edition
A C E F D B
Printed in the United States of America

Contents

Acknowledgments

Miranda Goes to Hollywood has been quite a journey. My mother and my friends were constant sources of support and encouragement. The exceptional women at McIntosh & Otis—Tracey Adams, Renee Cho, Dorothy Markinko, and Evva Pryor—are dedicated and resourceful, and I am enormously grateful to all of them. Rachel Myers copyedited the manuscript with astonishing precision, and I thank her.

To Karen Grove, my editor, who literally brought Miranda to life again, I owe more than words can ever express. She is meticulous and intuitive, and working with her is a joy.

I am thankful to Robert A. Harris and Joanne Lawson for their tireless and creative efforts on my behalf; to Leatrice Gilbert Fountain, who never lost faith; and to Kevin Brownlow, who is a kind and generous friend to those of us who love silent film. A special debt of gratitude goes to Charles and Joan Hull Turner for sharing the extraordinary letter that Joan's aunt, the

Oscar-winning actress Josephine Hull, wrote in 1913—recounting, with wit and charm, her five-day train trip across the country to a small, bucolic suburb of Los Angeles called Hollywood.

Author's Note

Although Miranda Gaines and The American Moving Picture Company are fictional, many of the people they encounter in the Hollywood of 1915 are not. I am a stickler for research, but I do believe it is the beginning and not the end—which is why I have blithely caused the fabled *Intolerance* sets to rise over the Fine Arts lot several months ahead of schedule. As journalist Adele Rogers St. Johns, who was there when Hollywood was young, was fond of saying: "If it didn't happen that way, it should have!"

One word about the culture of the era. In 1915 African Americans were called Negroes and coloreds (and worse), Native Americans were called Indians, and tobacco was used by the average citizen without knowledge of its harmful effects. To pretend otherwise would be dishonest.

Cast of Characters

The American Moving Picture Company

Miranda Gaines: A twelve-year-old orphan whose imaginative nature leads her to the moving picture game and adventure

Lucy Gaines: Piano teacher and seamstress, a woman whose practical demeanor disguises an independent streak as wide as her niece Miranda's

Bobby Gilmer: A boy of sixteen whose wisecracking independence masks a troubled spirit...or so he believes

C. J. Tourneur: A born director, opinionated, exasperating, and talented; a man loved as much for his faults as in spite of them

Jerry Donnelly: Irish to the bone, loyal, and sentimental; as fine a cameraman as ever cranked a Pathé

Mary Donnelly: The Company's costume mistress and surrogate mother, and the seldom-heeded voice of reason

Dulcie McGill: A lovely young actress who learns that innocence on-screen does not necessarily require innocence offscreen

Bessie McGill, a.k.a. **The Widow:** The charm of Caligula, the grace of a tractor—in short, a perfectly dreadful woman

Along the Way

Grover Johnson: An employee of the Pullman Company whose friendship with Miranda opens her eyes

Nate and the men in the baggage coach

In California

Jack Bell: Montana-born and -raised, a would-be actor who takes friendship seriously and the picture business with a large grain of salt

Zeb Calhoun: An ex-cowboy stunt director who takes one look at Lucy and decides he likes the view

Sullivan Randall (Sully): A Boston Brahmin so taken with the idea of Film as Art that he barely functions, except as an irritant

Thomas Ince and various employees of Inceville

Mack Sennett, Mabel Normand, Roscoe "Fatty" Arbuckle, and a carload of Keystone Cops

D. W. Griffith, Miss Lillian Gish, and various employees of the Fine Arts Studio

Wilbur Packer: Mayor of Cullersville, California

... and **Jake,** a small orange cat

Miranda Goes to Hollywood

Preface

From the September 23, 1914, issue of *Moving Picture News*:

> Word reaches our ears this week of yet another
> migration from these sodden and sullen shores:
> California-bound is The American Moving Pic-
> ture Company. Faithful readers will no doubt re-
> member the fine impression *Cupid and The Little
> Sister,* the company's premiere photoplay, made
> at Broadway's Astor Theatre during its August
> run. This scoop comes to *Moving Picture News* by
> way of the young company's Director General,
> Charles J. Tourneur—and we are not a bit sur-
> prised. Between the legal eagle eye of The Mo-
> tion Picture Patents Co., a.k.a. the Trust (see
> April 16 issue last), and our inclement climate,
> who can blame a fellow for packing up and head-
> ing west—lock, stock, and camera?

From Miranda Gaines to Robert Gilmer, dated October 7, 1914, written in pencil on sheets of lined paper
torn from a school copybook:

Dear Bobby,

I'm going to start this so by the time you send me your new address I'll have a whole letter written and ready to mail. Pardon the elegant stationery, but I'm writing this in class. After all the fun we had last summer making Cupid *and* The Little Sister, *sitting in a dusty old classroom and doing sums and parsing sentences and learning geography is torture. I'll just bet Mary Pickford doesn't know where Tierra del Fuego is.*

If Aunt Lucy doesn't hurry up and rent our house so we can come to California and I can be in the Company again with you and C.J. and Jerry and Mary and Dulcie, I think I'll just curl up and die.

I have to stop now, the teacher is staring at me.

             Miranda

From Charles James Tourneur to Miss Lucy Browning Gaines, dated October 9, 1914, written on the stationery of the Hollywood Hotel, in a dramatic looping hand. The letter is speckled with explosions of ink and droplets of coffee. From the ghostly imprint of a button on the last page, it also appears to have been blotted with a shirt sleeve:

My dear Miss Lucinda,

We have arrived!—no small miracle when one considers the cretins staffing the railroads these days. What an ordeal. How I remember dear old Bill Cody waxing rhapsodic (and endless) on The Great American Prairies. *Well, I have seen them, Lucinda—and he and every barroom balladeer from here to Missoula may have them. All the charm of Lear's blasted heath. Not that the lack of scenery*

2

prevented the passengers from popping up and down and running about and exclaiming over every little thing, behaving in general like headless chickens. You would think they had never seen rocks before. Small minds require small pleasures, I always say.

We are in residence at a grand hostelry, brimming to the very rafters with all manner of moving picture folk, and with comforts and services equal to the Waldorf or the old Hoffman House, bless the memory. We have taken a capacious apartment overlooking a range of rather unimaginative hills, which I am informed spring will improve no end. Then again, we are not here for the view.

As you may well imagine, I mourn separation from the lovely Dulcinea as utterly as I celebrate it from her gorgon of a mother. (What a mystery is genetics!) Bird in the hand, however, and the engagement in Fort Lee will keep her suitably— and profitably!—occupied until I arrange studio accommodations worthy of our endeavors.

Be strong, Lucinda. Stand firm against the narrow-minded peahens of Pine Street. Let them rot in that backwater where they belong—you and Miranda belong in this new and glorious world with us. Pack your trunk, strap Ridiculous Child to the top of the covered wagon, and get out here!

Give the delicious Miranda my heartfelt regards (or box her ears—I leave it to you) and be assured that I remain ever your devoted servant,

Charles James Tourneur, Esq.

From Robert Gilmer to Miranda Gaines, dated October 11, 1914, written on Hollywood Hotel stationery, in a precise, somewhat cramped hand. The pages are neatly blotted and folded around a brightly tinted postcard of the hotel:

Hello, Red!

I promised I'd write so here's a letter from yours truly, Star of Screen and Stage. Ha-ha, only kidding. We got here the day before yesterday after the all-time best trip ever. We all had berths, too, so no sitting up all night in day coach. I've been on trains before (about half my life, I think sometimes), but this was the first time all the way across the country "in one take," so to speak. The West is fantastic! It looks just like a Tom Mix picture, I swear.

I won't say any more because I want you to see it with a fresh eye. I will say (and you know better than to tell Miss Lucy, right?) that Jerry and Mary and I got so darned fed up with C.J. only the thought of prison stopped us from tossing him off the back of the train. My guess is he's just nervous about starting over again when we barely got started before, but jeez, can that man complain! The food was too hot, the food was too cold, his berth was lumpy, and (my personal favorite) there was sand coming in the window when we went through the desert. What did he expect—feathers? Good thing he's a great director or nobody would put up with him for more than about five minutes.

This hotel is one deluxe trap. Too bad we only have two tiny rooms on the top floor in the back. C.J. claims that in a week or so we'll move to "digs befitting our status." Honestly! Meanwhile, you can barely get into the Donnellys' room because of Jerry's equipment. He's still afraid the Trust is going to find us and smash everything, and after the close call we had in August, I can't say I blame him. But if he doesn't quit shoving poor Baby in the closet every time he hears a noise in the corridor, she'll start spitting parts and then where'll we be? The only picture company in town without a camera, that's where. And Mary has her sewing machine and her manikins and all our costumes in there, too. Those two never heard of traveling light.

You don't have to be a genius at mathematics to figure out what that means. I'm sharing a room with The Boss. Some fun. Clothes where he drops them, magazines all over the floor, and he snores like a wounded buffalo. Not to mention that he's a real chimney with those rotten Caporals of his. I've collected two complete sets of White Sox cards, but half the time I can't breathe. So mostly I sit on the porch and read or listen to all the actors who live here lie about what big cheeses they are.

I know you can keep secrets so here's another one. The Boss still owes me money from Cupid, and he says until we rent a studio he'll give me an allowance. Like I was his kid, perish the thought. I've only been earning my own living since I was thirteen, for cripes' sake, and being on the dole gives me the fidgets something awful.

Well, that's it for now. I never had anyone to write to, and it's not half bad. Write me back, okay?

Sincerely,

Bobby

5

Miranda's letter is continued:

Dear Bobby,

I'm supposed to be doing my homework, but I have to tell you the latest on Emma Duncan, the Terror of Pine Street. You remember how nasty she was to me about being in Cupid and how mean she was to Auntie? I still don't see how she could blame her for letting me go to hell in a handcart when she didn't even know I was making the picture (Auntie, I mean), but Old Lady Duncan is what you would call a stinker.

Last week, after you all left, she made her move! I'll just bet she decided to wait until C.J. wasn't here to kiss all the ladies' hands and say they should be on the stage. Anyway, she hauls the Leewood Heights Benevolent Society, minus Auntie, over to her house for a war council. (Jimmy and Tommy and I hid in the closet under the stairs and heard every word.) But the ladies said why was she carping about sinful moving pictures when she had never even seen one? So they all got dressed up and went into New York City to see Cupid.

Guess what? They loved it! I wish I could have seen Old Lady Duncan's face when she showed up in the streetcar scene. Remember the day we shot the chase and she caught me and we had that big fight and C.J. kept it in? I'll bet she pitched a fit, the way Auntie did when we went to the picture show for my birthday and they ran Cupid because Quo Vadis? burned up in the projection booth and she found out I was in the picture. She says now she would have let me, so I wasted all that time sneaking around like a criminal—but that's not what she said then!

6

Mrs. Stowing told Auntie if that's what moving pictures were like she was going to open a picture show herself so she could go all the time. And Mrs. Fellowes came over Sunday with a seven-layer chocolate that she baked just for me!!! She told me the part where The Boy (I mean you) almost gets hanged made her cry harder than the part in Ben-Hur where his mother and sister get leprosy. I've got to read that book now, I didn't know there were lepers in it.

I'd better stop before Auntie comes upstairs and finds me not memorizing state capitals. More later—

I'm supposed to be in bed, so I'll finish this quickly before you-know-who sees my light on. C.J.'s letter came today so now I have your address. After what he said about the trip, I guess all his carrying on about the wide-open spaces and the old pioneer spirit must be just talk. The hotel sounds wonderful, though. I can't wait to eat in the dining room every night. My idea of heaven on earth is to never wash another dish as long as I live.

Did you write to me yet? I asked the mailman and he said California wasn't next door and I should be patient. That should make you laugh. Me being patient, I mean.

Very truly yours,

Miranda

P.S. The Pine Street Irregulars met after school today, and I drew to an inside straight and won Tommy's best aggie off him. You would have been proud of me. I really miss you.

Telegram from Miss L. B. Gaines, 34 Pine Street, Leewood Heights, New Jersey, to Mr. C. J. Tourneur c/o

The Hollywood Hotel, Hollywood Boulevard, Hollywood, California; dated December 10, 1914:

> AFFAIRS HERE SETTLED STOP DEPART NEW
> YORK 20 DECEMBER STOP ARRIVE 24 DECEMBER
> ARCADE STREET STATION LOS ANGELES 6:45 PM
> STOP PLEASE BOOK ROOM AND WIRE CONFIR-
> MATION STOP REGARDS LUCY GAINES

By return wire:

> LUCINDA DEAREST AWAIT YOUR ARRIVAL WITH
> BATED BREATH AND GREATEST POSSIBLE EX-
> CITEMENT STOP WILL MEET TRAIN STOP AUF
> WIEDERSEHEN AND MERRY CHRISTMAS STOP CJ

The Old World

It was as cold and gray a day as Miranda could remember, the sky a flat low sheet of steel over Manhattan. The wind came off the Hudson River in fierce angry bursts, sending hats flying and flinging pedestrians into doorways like scraps before a broom. Travelers driven by haste and purpose, and the punishing wind, rushed with collars up and heads down through the great bronze doors of Pennsylvania Station. Here, where travels began and journeys ended amid the vast gloomy grandeur of a cathedral, the noise was never ending—a ceaseless thrumming surf rising to the fretwork of steel and glass roofing the Concourse, echoing through wide marble arcades and off the looming pillars of stone in the Waiting Room, spilling and clattering down the long, lamplit stairways to the platforms.

The train to Chicago stood in readiness, festive with light, her platform crowded. Splashes of color shone bright as confetti against the soot-grimed walls and underground gloom: feathers gleaming on hats, here and there the rich luster of fur, woolen mufflers in vivid shades of crimson and blue and green, armfuls of gaily wrapped packages. Baggage carts breasted the crowd, porters hoarsely shouting, "Make way, make way." Newsboys lithe as eels wriggled and darted, their cries of, "Extra! Extra! Huns pushed back!" ringing shrill above the tears, laughter, and last-minute instructions of a hundred partings.

Miranda and Lucy Gaines leaned out the window of their compartment, straining to spot the Leewood Heights delegation amid the sea of fluttering handkerchiefs. Lucy kept dabbing her eyes, waving her handkerchief only once or twice. Miranda waved her hat vigorously and, when Lucy's head was turned, blew kisses to the crowd.

At a signal, the conductor swung smartly up onto the steps behind the engine. He lifted his head, cupped a hand to his mouth, and bellowed:

"Bo-o-o-ard! All a-bo-o-o-a-a-ard!"

The whistle sounded, a terrifying, thrilling shriek, and the train jerked, rocked, then steadied itself as the wheels began to move along the rails. Slowly, ponderously, groaning under its own weight, *The Empire State* pulled out of the terminal.

"Shut the window, darling, or we'll be covered with cinders in no time," Lucy said. She wiped her eyes again and tucked her handkerchief in her sleeve with an air of finality.

"In a minute, Auntie. I want one last look at the city."

"With the window shut. Now."

"Yes'm. Look, there's—oh, it's gone now."

"Hmm?" said Lucy distractedly, as she rooted through her purse.

"The Woolworth Building, I think," said Miranda. "It was the tallest one, anyhow."

"Sky like flint and cold to freeze the bones," Lucy said, looking up briefly. "What a day."

"Good day to leave," Miranda said. *We're leaving,* she thought. *We're actually leaving. I can't believe it.* She thought of Jerry Donnelly, and pictured him setting off from Belfast, armed with only a knapsack and talent. Jerry referred to anything on the far side of the Atlantic as the Old World. Maybe he meant more than distance. Maybe the Old World was whatever you left behind.

She bounced experimentally on the brown plush seat. "Kind of hard for sleeping. Slippery, too."

"They open up, the berths are underneath," Lucy said. She slid out the hatpin and removed her hat, and began rearranging the blond waves brushing her forehead. "And how many times do I have to tell you, pull the back of your skirt down before you sit," she said, squinting into a pocket mirror as she poked at a stubborn curl. "Oh, why did I let that woman marcelle my hair? This is giving me the jimjams."

Lucy had dictated they travel In Style. She was an accomplished seamstress—indeed, for years she had augmented the money she made teaching piano with dressmaking—but a journey of this magnitude called for at least one perfect store-bought outfit. She had chosen well, and her gray traveling suit with the fashionable peg-top skirt flattered both her neat, slightly plump figure and her delicate coloring. Miranda's wide-collared dress of dark green was equally becoming to her red hair and dark brown eyes, and was trimmed with bands of Russian embroidery at the hem and cuffs. This did not, thought Miranda, compensate for either the tightness of the armholes or the scratchiness of the wool. She had lost the argument in the shoe store as well. "Twelve-year-olds do not wear high heels," Lucy had decreed, rejecting Miranda's choice—parrot green silk pumps with enormous paste buckles—for a depressingly ordinary pair of black kid boots, laced up and low heeled.

There was a knock on the door. Lucy said, "Enter"—and the door was opened by a tall black man with a broad face. His white cotton jacket was shiny with boiled starch, the crease in his black trousers could have sliced bread, and his shoes were buffed to mirrors. The brass plaque on his black forage cap read: PULLMAN COMPANY.

"Miss Gaines? Afternoon, ma'am. Name's Grover Johnson," he said. His voice was deep, his manner and bearing formal. "I'll be lookin' after you this trip. I understand y'all will be traveling with us past Chicago."

"All the way to California!"

"You must be Miss Miranda," he said, and smiled at her before returning his attention to Lucy. "You know about tomorrow mornin', Miss Gaines?"

"The change at Union Station?"

"Yes, ma'am. We pick up The California Limited there. You'll have two hours' wait. Most folks like to have lunch in town, stretch their legs some. I tend to the bags, so you needn't worry yourself." He handed

12

her a stiff white card the size of a song sheet and said, "Dinner menu, ma'am. It's set for tonight, but on *The Limited* you can order like a restaurant. We got Harvey service so there'll be fine eats all the way out. Fresh strawberries and 'nilla ice cream suit the young lady?"

"Strawberries in December? I'll say!"

"Now, don't hesitate," he said. "Anything you need just do that little button there on the wall, or ask anyone for Grover." The door closed soundlessly, and he was gone.

"What a nice man," said Miranda. "I don't think I ever talked to a Negro before." Lucy looked at her sharply, and she said, "Well, where was I supposed to meet them? There weren't any at school, or in church, or even on our side of town."

Lucy was silent for a moment. "Perhaps it's time you knew more of this world than one small town," she said seriously. "And you will call him Mr. Johnson. I will not have you referring to your elders by their first names."

"I call C.J. and Jerry by their first names."

"The rules of polite society may not apply to those two, but they do apply to you."

"Yes'm. What're we having for dinner?"

Lucy frowned at the menu—the type had been selected more for elegance of design than readability—then fetched her wire-rimmed spectacles from her purse and hooked them on. "Good heavens! This is more like your mama and papa's trip on the Hamburg Line than what I expected on a train. Gigot of Lamb, Asparagus with Sauce Hollandaise. Whatever do you suppose Consommé à la Royale is?"

Miranda bounced on the seat. "I believe I'm going to like travel."

"The train bounces enough," Lucy said mildly. "You needn't add to it."

"Oh, Auntie, dearest Auntie, do you think maybe tonight I could try one teeny little sip of champagne? Just to see what all the fuss is about," she added quickly.

"Absolutely not! If alcohol so much as touches your lips before your twenty-first birthday, I guarantee you'll not live to see it."

"I was only asking," Miranda said defensively. The angle of Lucy's jaw signaled a change of subject. "I still can't believe everyone came to see us off, Auntie, can you? Even Mrs. Duncan. And after all those things she said about me being more dangerous than a Bolshevik and you letting me go to hell in a handcart."

"There are some things I shall miss about Leewood Heights," Lucy said, "and some I shall not. What did Jimmy give you? I saw him shove something into your hand just before we boarded."

"His best Indian arrowhead," Miranda said. "And Tommy gave me his favorite cat's-eye marble and a bullet from his father's pistol for good-luck charms. I guess I'll never see them again," she added, her chin quivering dangerously. "Probably not as long as I live."

"Some adventuress you are," Lucy said lightly. "All I've heard for months now is California, California, California. Oh well, if you want to go back, I'll ring Mr. Johnson and have our bags taken off at the next station." She rose from her seat and reached for the call button.

14

"Auntie, no!" Miranda grabbed for Lucy's arm. "I didn't mean—oh, you're teasing me."

"Oh, darling girl, I was just trying to stem the waterworks. I could not bear one more tear this day."

"We *are* doing the right thing, aren't we?" Miranda whispered. Suddenly, and only for the most fleeting of moments, there was an empty feeling under her ribs that made her want to lie down somewhere and shut her eyes.

"I hope so," Lucy said. "I certainly hope so." She patted Miranda on the knee. "Listen, I cannot face the idea of unpacking—although I must say all these cunning little drawers and cupboards are a temptation— so why don't we go exploring? I imagine we can get a soda pop in the club car."

"And maybe take a look out the back?"

"Remember what we discussed? No hanging out open windows, no leaning out between cars, and *no* unchaperoned trips to the back platform."

"For Pete's sake, you're not going to follow me around the whole time, are you? I won't get into trouble."

"Now where," Lucy said with a raised eyebrow, "have I heard that before?"

The reference was specific, and uncomfortable. *"Stay away from those people,"* Lucy had warned Miranda at the beginning of the summer. Pine Street had been invaded, the insular and very ordinary nature of the quiet tree-lined block shattered by the strangers who had rented the house next door, built an open stage in the adjoining vacant lot, and were blissfully— and noisily—making flickers.

"Actors," sniffed Emma Duncan, "are trash. No decent woman would have them in her home, speak to them on the street, or allow her children near them."

"Promise me you'll stay away," Lucy had commanded, reluctantly casting her lot with the dreadnoughts for the sake of peace and income.

"Yes, Auntie," Miranda had promised sweetly, fingers crossed behind her back. "I won't get into trouble."

Miranda grinned wickedly, then mirrored Lucy's expression and lifted eyebrow. "Why, Auntie, dearest, whatever do you mean?" *And if I'd kept my word like a Goody Two-shoes,* she thought complacently, *I'd never have met the Company or been in* Cupid, *and we wouldn't be going all the way across the entire United States on a train.*

All during the long months of autumn Miranda had imagined every detail of the trip west, creating scenario after scenario as she went through the motions of home, school, homework, chores. Here was Miranda boarding the train in Pennsylvania Station, resplendent in velvet cloak and plumed hat, arms dripping jewels as she tossed roses to an adoring crowd.... Here were Tommy Stowing and Jimmy Duncan, dressed as Pinkerton detectives with bowler hats and cigars, forcing Old Lady Duncan—at gunpoint, of course!—to kiss the hem of Miranda's garment.... Here was Miranda holding court on the train, entertaining the passengers with tales of the moving-picture game until dawn rose over the Great Prairies. Here, in short, was Miranda Gaines staying up all night and doing exactly as she pleased.

Fantasies are just that—not even a perpetual

dreamer like Miranda expected more—but December 20, 1914, had come satisfyingly close. There had been a large crowd at the station, Emma Duncan had shed unbecoming tears, and it had been lovely to sit in a deep overstuffed armchair in the club car, sipping sarsaparilla while the landscape rolled snowy and serene past the window. But by the time Miranda was halfway through their dining-car feast, it was apparent she wouldn't see midnight, let alone the dawn. With quiet amusement, Lucy led her back to the compartment. The berths were made up and turned down, the shades were drawn, and the bedside reading lamps were lit. It was too snug and inviting a nest for anything but sleep, and it was a mumbling, stumbling Miranda who allowed herself to be undressed and tucked in as she had not for years.

She awoke at dawn to the alarming sensation that the room was all wrong. The window was at her feet instead of to her right, and it was too small and shaped funny. Where was the elm tree, and the lovely old climbing roses that rubbed against her windowpane? Where was the lace canopy overhead, the first thing she saw every waking morning of her life? Then the noise of the wheels rose up, and she remembered. A wave of homesickness swept over her. She turned on her side and wrapped her arms around the pillow.... She was in her bedroom on Pine Street. Lucy was downstairs playing the piano, and the curtains drifted on a warm summer breeze. There was her window seat with the faded cretonne cushion and the row of dolls, and Tommy was standing in the yard with his mitt and ball, calling for her to come out and play. She fell asleep running barefoot in the grass, the pillow damp beneath her cheek.

Chicago was a disappointment. "This looks like New York," Miranda said smugly, "only not as big." She had a similar reaction to a hurried pass through the Art Institute. "You don't have nearly as many paintings as the Metropolitan Museum of Art, you know," she informed one of the guards, who did not seem impressed by the information. Her excitement returned when they reboarded, however. *The California Limited*, on the Santa Fe Railroad! If that didn't sound like the way west, what did?

Sleep was impossible that night. The previous night Miranda dismissed, with remembered embarrassment, as behavior unsuited to a seeker of adventure. *How could a train lull you to sleep*, she thought impatiently, *when the train itself never slept?* The darkness was alive with sound: the endless *chook-a-tah, chook-a-tah* of the wheels, the hollow clatter over a dry wash or the humming echo over water, then the return to the familiar rhythm as the wheels rejoined solid railbed; the creaking of the berths, the bobbled curtain fringe tapping against the windows, the spigot dripping into the basin; the mysterious footsteps in the corridor.

Alert to every nuance of Lucy's breathing, Miranda slid out of bed and into her new dressing gown and slippers. *Auntie must think we're going to Alaska instead of California*, she thought as she knotted the cord around her waist; the robe was of the heaviest grade outing flannel and lined. She tiptoed out into the corridor, crept through the silent and empty stateroom cars and down along the center aisles of the sleepers.

She proceeded cautiously, careful to step around the shoes set out for polishing in front of each curtained berth, intent on stealth and silence.

Miranda reached the club car at the rear of the train and peered through the glass door. The car was dark, but she could see a single muted circle of light over the bar. Grover was standing behind the counter, humming to himself and polishing glasses. She opened the door, and he looked up.

"Why, hello there, Miss Miranda. What you up to wandering 'round in the small hours?"

"I'm not sure, Mr. Johnson. I couldn't sleep."

"Know what you mean," he said with a smile. "Train when folks's sleeping belongs to those who ain't. Have a seat and keep me company." Miranda climbed onto a stool and propped her elbows on the bar. Grover slid a bowl toward her. "Goobers," he said. Miranda nibbled and watched the cloth in his hand circle the glass. The silence between them was comfortable. Grover held the glass to the light, nodded, set it in a rack under the counter, and picked up another.

"Mind a question?"

Miranda shook her head (her mouth was full).

"You seem mighty excited about gettin' to California. What's out there got you so het up?"

She swallowed and wiped her mouth on her sleeve. "I am going to Los Angeles," she said with enunciation worthy of C.J., "to be an actress with The American Moving Picture Company."

"Little bitty thang like you? I swan."

"It's true. I was already in a picture called *Cupid and The Little Sister*. Did you see it?"

19

"Don't generally have time for picture shows," Grover answered diplomatically. "But I'm sure I'd like it. We've had plenty picture folk on *The Limited*. Fellow calls hisself Turner or somesuch came through few months back. Puffed-up little gent, loud as all get-out."

Miranda froze with a handful of peanuts halfway to her mouth, then giggled and said, "Sounds like a director. My friend Bobby says they all have loud voices from screaming at actors."

"Bosses is bosses the world over," he said amiably. "I ain't never found different."

"Do you have a family, Mr. Johnson?"

"Nice of you to ask. Yes'm, I do. They're back home, little town in Alabama you never heard of. Don't see 'em but once a month. Like to see a picture? Had it took special over to Gadsden," he said proudly. Miranda nodded, and he took his wallet from inside his jacket and extracted a small tissue-wrapped packet. He slid out the sepia-tinted photograph and handed it to Miranda. The picture was glued to a cardboard mount with the studio name stamped in gilt across a corner.

The woman was wearing a plain black dress, a bar pin glinting at the high collar. Her hair was scraped back into a bun, and there was a severe expression on her high-cheekboned face. One arm was around a boy of twelve in a knickers suit, who stared solemnly into the camera. His sister, who looked no older than six, was nestled against her mother's shoulder, wearing a white ruffled dress. Her dimpled smile was a replica of Grover's.

"What are their names?" Miranda asked.

"My wife's named Emily. Then there's Grover, Junior. Smart as a whip, that boy. Wants to be an animal doctor. He's allus takin' in stray dogs and cats and patchin' 'em up. And that's Cissy. She's my baby."

"You must miss them something awful," Miranda said softly. She handed Grover the photograph, and he kissed it unashamedly before putting it away.

He picked up a glass and cleared his throat. "You ready to go out back? See the stars from the open?"

"Can I?" Miranda said eagerly. "I mean, may I?"

"May I," Grover chuckled. "Why else you come all the way back here?" He pulled down a thick green wool blanket from an overhead cabinet and handed it to her. "Wrap up good now. You catch pneumonia, Miss Lucy'll have my hide."

Miranda folded the blanket around her head and shoulders. "There," she said. "Do I look like an Apache?"

"Got the braids for it and nothin' else. Now don't stay too long. And don't fall off," he called after her. "I need this job."

Miranda stood on the platform and watched the rails spin away into the dark. The whistle sounded, long and deep and mournful in the sharp air—they were passing a town some miles away, a scattered bracelet of light on the horizon.

Perhaps it was Grover's photograph, or perhaps it was simply being alone with the night, but Miranda found herself thinking about her mother and father. They had been dead for many years now, the spirited pretty woman with the cloud of auburn hair and the tall shy man who had spoken seldom and smiled often, and her memories of them had grown as dim as the pictures slowly turning silver in Lucy's albums. She had never been able to imagine them among the clouds and seraphim of Sunday-school heaven or sense them in the low, tree-hemmed sky at home. Now, looking at the black eternal sky above, she understood how something could be faraway and close at the same time. Maybe they were up there after all, as fixed and constant as the stars in their nocturnal dance, while the wheels far below tore across the miles.

The wind had a metallic harshness to it and smelled of wet earth and wood smoke and snow. She leaned into it until her face burned with the cold.

I will remember this for the rest of my life, she thought. *I will remember the night and the stars and the wind on my face. I'm Miranda Gaines, and I know where I'm going.*

Where the Rails Meet the Sky

The rolling farmlands of Iowa were behind them. The Missouri had been crossed, the long bridge into Omaha dividing East from West as cleanly as a line on a map. Miranda had pressed her nose to the window and imagined pioneers and covered wagons and—even though she knew it was the wrong river— Huck and Jim, heading for freedom on a raft. Lucy's thoughts had been of crossing the Rubicon, and she had whispered to herself, "The die is cast."

Lucy had earmarked the afternoon for the observation car and a minister's wife from Peoria who promised several new fancy knitting stitches. They were settled in with their workbags and a pot of tea, chatting away like old friends amid a cozy welter of yarn and needles and instruction pamphlets. Miranda sat with them for a while, but her impatience increased with every mile: You could knit any old time— how often could you see real prairies? There was something hypnotic about the flat endlessness of Nebraska, as though they were on a great ship steaming through seas of golden grass. The herds of sheep trailing like spilled paint along the gentle rises in the land were foam edging the rolling waves, every distant man on a horse was a lonely fisherman in a dinghy, and the far-flung towns rose like islands.

"Auntie, look!" Miranda exclaimed. "Look at that man—see? Tying up his horse there? He just has to be a cowboy."

"Yes, dear," Lucy said distractedly. "Two, four, six . . . here's the problem. I dropped a stitch."

The minister's wife laughed at Miranda's expression and said kindly, "It's not a bad way to pass the time, child. I could teach you, if you'd like."

"No, thank you," Miranda said politely. "I've tried before and all I ever get is these knotty lumps I can't get the needles through. I'll just watch the— Oh no!"

"What now," Lucy said, her eyes on her hands.

"It's *snowing*. Now I can't see a thing."

"Miranda—," Lucy said darkly.

"I'm going to get a book," said Miranda. "This is giving me the pip."

She was halfway to the compartment when she remembered she had packed every last book in her trunk in the blithe certainty she would need no more entertainment than the trip itself. "Rats," she muttered. "Why didn't I save *The Prince and the Pauper* for my suitcase? I've only read it twice." With the single-mindedness of the inveterate reader in search of something—anything!—to read, she made her way to the baggage coach at the front of the train.

The door was marked EMPLOYEES ONLY. Miranda took a deep breath, opened the door . . . and was seized by a fit of coughing. The air was blue with smoke and rank with the odor of cigarettes and cheap cigars. The car was dark and unwindowed, the only source of light an oil lantern swaying from the ceiling. Miranda began to work along the narrow aisle between the walls of baggage, trying to decipher luggage tags and labels in the gloom. As she neared the center of the car, the smoke thickened, and she heard voices. She crept forward, caught the toe of her shoe in the handle of a portmanteau, and fell sprawling into a pool of light.

Quickly, she scrambled to her feet. Seven Pullman porters were staring at her. They were seated on suitcases pulled up around a large leather-covered trunk belonging to a doctor from Philadelphia, the top of which was littered with heaps of coins, crumpled bills, overflowing ashtrays, and playing cards.

"He-hello, Mr. Johnson," Miranda said, fastening on the one welcoming face. "I just came to get a book from my trunk. I didn't mean to interrupt you, honest."

"You ain't s'pose to be in here," said one of the men.

"You listen to Nate now," a gray-headed man added sourly. "It don't do to mess in our bid'ness."

Miranda glanced at the trunk and saw that four nines and a king were fanned faceup beside the largest pile of money. "What're you doing?" she asked.

"What does it look like we're doin'," Nate growled.

"Playin' cards, mister?" Miranda said sweetly, twisting her braid around a finger. Bobby's voice sounded in her head: *Don't overplay the scene, Red.*

"Easy, Nate," Grover said. "She's a nice enough gal, let her stay. You set here, Miss Miranda." He patted his suitcase and winked at her.

Nate gathered the cards and shuffled them. "Just so's you know, li'l girl," he said in a patronizing tone, "this here game's called poker."

"Draw or stud?" Miranda said coolly, and flipped her braid over her shoulder.

There was a pause, then the men started laughing. Nate, to his credit, laughed the loudest. "Hell's bells," said one. "Deal her in."

Miranda folded her first two hands, discreetly watching the pattern of raises and calls as Bobby had taught her the previous summer. After she won the third pot with two pairs, jacks over eights—a cow-town classic known as deadman's hand—Nate began calling her Jersey Red. Her pile of silver and bills had grown nicely after an hour, although the morose little gray-headed man was convinced she was a midget run away from the carny, and said so repeatedly. Grover, however, was tickled to bits. On learning that Miranda had been taught by an actor (notorious cardsharps, it seemed), he launched into a colorful and somewhat confused account of the time Maurice Barrymore was shot in a barroom brawl over a hand of cards, or maybe it was a woman—whereupon Miranda sprang to her feet in a panic.

"What time is it?" she cried.

Seven hands went into pockets. Seven nickel-plated railroad watches were drawn forth and clicked open. Seven voices intoned, "Three twenty-one."

"Auntie's gonna kill me for sure," Miranda said, scraping her winnings into her skirt pocket. "I'm sorry, I have to leave. 'Bye, Mr. Johnson, 'bye Nate. Thanks ever so much, but I'd better go." She started for the door, then turned and tossed her last hand onto the trunk lid. As she ran for the door, she heard Nate say, "That durn kid. Lookee here, boys! Three deuces and a pair o' ladies."

A quick peek into the observation car told her Lucy and the minister's wife were still in pursuit of the perfect cable. Miranda went directly to their compartment, emptied her pocket onto the pull-down writing table, and set about tallying up her winnings. The total was inspiringly high. She was contemplating her outstretched foot, turning it this way and that to admire the imaginary three-inch heels and glittery paste buckles, when a finger tapped her lightly on the shoulder and a familiar voice said, "This looks interesting."

Miranda jumped up and knocked her elbow against the writing desk, which sprang back into the wall with a bang. The money went flying in a silvery, clattering spray.

"Pick it up," said Lucy, seating herself. "Then tell me where it came from."

The Denver Mint would be my guess, Miranda thought crossly, as she bent down to chase a dime that had rolled out of sight.

"Here." Lucy stabbed a forefinger at the seat, then folded her hands calmly in her lap.

Miranda dumped the money into a heap, then sat on the opposite berth. She cleared her throat into the silence and said, "Poker."

"I see," Lucy said calmly. "With whom, if you don't mind my asking."

"Mr. Johnson and his friends, but it's not their fault so you shouldn't blame them. I barged into their game in the baggage coach when I went to look for—"

"Miranda Louise Gaines, you have been *gambling*." Lucy's voice was shaking with rage. "I will not have it. Do you hear me? I will not have it. The devil's pasteboards, at your age."

"But you and your friends play cards all the time." *The devil's pasteboards?* she thought. *I'll bet you got that one from Old Lady Duncan.*

"There is a world of difference between whist in the parlor and gambling for money. What has come over you, Miranda? I raised you better than—" Lucy's eyes narrowed and she drummed her fingers on the seat. "This is that Gilmer boy's doing, isn't it?"

Miranda stared at her. "I thought you liked Bobby."

"I do like him. I think he's a miracle of common sense and good manners considering his upbringing, but he is older than you and—"

"Only four years," Miranda protested.

"It might as well be forty for all that boy has seen and done. I should have known something like this would happen. He has altogether too much of an influence on you."

"He's the best friend I ever had," Miranda said fiercely.

"I know, darling, I know," Lucy said quietly. "But he should not have taught you to gamble, and I plan on telling him so. For now, you will start by returning that money."

"But . . . they said it was just their tips."

"Did it occur to you that those men live, for the most part, on gratuities? How they handle their income is their business, but I will not have you taking money from them in any fashion. It's more than manners, honey. It's common decency."

"I bet they won't take it back. I won it on the square."

"Then tell them to donate it to the Association of Retired Sleeping Car Porters or something. Go now, this minute, before I lose all patience."

They were out of Nebraska by morning. Wyoming lay before them, an immense reach of frozen earth and twisted rock, splotched with scudding cloud shadows, barren and beautiful beneath a pale winter sky. It was the western scenery of Miranda's dreams—and she barely noticed.

She stared at her reflection in the window, hiding her face from Lucy as she nibbled her fingernails and fretted. *What if she tries to keep us apart?* she thought frantically. *If she's decided Bobby's a bad influence... maybe I can warn him. Oh, how can I? I'm stuck on this blasted train. Two more days. I'll explode. I'll die. I'll—*

"Look, darling, mountains!" Lucy exclaimed.

"Uh-huh. Very nice."

The countryside was growing wilder by the mile, harsh and raw and unforgiving. Snaggle-toothed cairns of rock towered higher and higher on either side of the train as they neared the blue-and-white mountains, sharply defined against the soaring sky. There was a slender cleft at the base of the mountains, and the train snaked through into Echo Canyon. The canyon passage was narrow and twisting, following alongside the path of a swift furious river, dark and clear where the icy mountain water eddied into pools, white with froth where it broke and ran over jagged stones. They slid beneath ocher and brown cliffs pockmarked with cave entrances, then blinked in and out of a series of short tunnels and emerged in Weber Canyon— broader, less dangerous-looking, the mountains less immediate. The Utah border brought orchards and tidy little farms, prosperous-looking small towns, and a definite drop in the excitement level.

"Is that a—? Oh, it couldn't be," said Lucy. "I don't believe it. Look, darling, seagulls!"

"California already?"

"No, silly, the Great Salt Lake. I'm going to go freshen up, and I suggest you do the same. We have almost an hour in Salt Lake City."

"If I sent a telegram to everyone would it get to California by tomorrow? I thought it might be kind of exciting—I've never sent one before."

"I don't see why not," Lucy replied, clearly amused. "But keep it to ten words, darling. They're cheaper that way."

Lucy would have not been amused, however, by the message Miranda penned to Bobby, cupping her hand around the printed form for privacy:

CAUGHT PLAYING POKER STOP DO ORPHAN
ACT FOR AUNTIE TOMORROW STOP RED

That should do it, Miranda thought with spirit-lifting relief. Bobby could play the wistful young hero better than any Biograph juvenile. Hadn't he proved just that in *Cupid and The Little Sister? I'm a goose for worrying*, she thought. *Everything will be fine and dandy once we get there.*

By evening they had climbed out of the flatlands into mining country. Campfires flickered across the darkening hills like fireflies, and Miranda caught her first glimpse of sagebrush in the coppery glow of the setting sun. They crossed into Nevada in the night, awakening to the high noon glare of a desert sun. The temperature rose alarmingly, and Grover brought a block of ice for their cooling cabinet and set the electric fan blowing across it. The morning was spent with the curtains and blinds drawn against the unseasonable heat, Miranda cracking the blinds occasionally to watch the mesmerizing repetition of sand, sagebrush, rocks, cactus, sand, sagebrush, rocks, cactus.

"Now I know where the middle of nowhere is," she remarked. "The prairies were lonely, but they were so clean looking. Can you imagine living here?"

The towns—if they qualified as such—were of a dreary sameness: a few poor shacks with tin-can chimneys, chickens pecking sadly at the dirt, a dry-goods store and a saloon, a smattering of cowboys and ranchers, a handful of Mexicans and Indians.

Then they struck genuine desert, all blinding sand and shimmering heat, nearly bereft of vegetation, the mountains a distant brown crust folded along the rim of the earth. "This is amazing country," Lucy said, patting her temples with a cologne-dampened handkerchief. "Just when you think you've seen the emptiest landscape imaginable it changes again, and there you are!—a whole new kind of empty."

After an hour, the desert yielded, and the first sighting of drab greenish scrub was as welcome as crocuses through snow. The towns reappeared, as dusty and forlorn as before. There was a knock, and Grover put his head around the door. "Thought Miss Miranda might like to know, ma'am, we passed into California a few minutes back."

"This?" Miranda jerked her thumb at the window. "This is the garden spot everyone's always squawkin' about?"

"Miranda, your manners!" Lucy said.

"It pretties up soon enough," Grover said. "Now, if you ladies'll pass on lunch in the dining car and come to the rear with me, you'll see somethin' most folks miss."

They followed him, weaving politely through corridors crowded with diners heading upstream. The single occupant of the club car, an elderly gentleman nose-deep in the morning paper, Grover dispatched with the information that maybe the fresh rainbow trout on the luncheon menu wouldn't last until the second sitting. He then took his post behind the bar and gestured them onto the padded leather stools. Lucy perched cautiously, Miranda with a casual air that ill concealed her excitement.

"Provisions, ladies," Grover said, as he set out a plate of chicken sandwiches and a dish of bread-and-butter pickles.

"What's going to happen, Mr. Johnson?" Miranda asked.

"Wait, wait," said Grover, his eyes on his watch. "Best park them sandwiches... *now*. Here we go!"

The whistle screamed its earsplitting call—and

they were plunged into inky darkness, as immediate as the extinguishing of a candle flame, and surrounded by a great booming rush of noise. Grover waited for a few seconds to heighten the effect, then fumbled for the lamp over the bar and switched it on. "Tunnel," he shouted. "Longest one. Finish up, then we're going out back for the coop dee grass."

They followed Grover down the length of the car, and he opened the door out onto the little railed platform where Miranda had watched the stars. The sound of the train struck their ears like hammer blows, and they edged out onto the swaying platform and immediately grabbed the railing for balance.

The tunnel had been blasted from the living mountain with little room to spare, and the roof was oppressively low. The jagged walls were black with soot and cinders, and oozed damp. The noise, which had nowhere to go but back in on itself, was overwhelming. Just when Miranda thought she could stand no more and must flee inside or scream, the darkness lifted and the train burst into sunlight.

They were halfway to the sky, racing along a cut on the face of a mountain. Behind them the dark maw of the tunnel receded. Miranda and Lucy turned to look down the side of the mountain, and there, spread before them like a Persian carpet, were the canyons and mountains of the Los Angeles Basin, as green in winter as a New England spring. In the far distance the Pacific Ocean was barely visible as a glimmering thread of blue on the horizon.

"My Lord," Lucy gasped. "Oh, that air feels good. It's so clean, so cool."

"And the sky!" said Miranda. "Did you ever see such a sky? Oh, thank you, Mr. Johnson, thank you. I wouldn't have missed this for the world."

"Finest leg of the run, to my mind," Grover stated. "It's always a treat, but it's extra pretty what with this warm spell."

"It's not always like this?" said Miranda.

"Oh, no. More like March back East, coldish and damp. This year's been rare. We'll no doubt fry come summer," he replied. "I'd best be back to my duties now, but you stay while you've got the view to yourselves."

The Limited wound down through the mountains, the parched throats and brassy skies of the morning fading like a nightmare on waking. As the altitude dropped, flowers appeared, wild gentians and columbine, and Michaelmas daisies—and poppies. Years before some botany-minded railroad employee had thrown poppy seeds from the train, and they had seeded and reseeded to a great golden-yellow mass banking the rails, bowing to the rush of the train, lifting their heads to the sun in its wake.

"It's a river of gold," Lucy said in a hushed voice. "Like a path straight to heaven."

At sea level the mountains receded to a smoky silhouette. The truck farms and vineyards of the slopes gave way to mile upon mile of orchards in bloom, a downy white counterpane spread back to the base of the hills, the land as flat as the prairies but with none of their desolation. "What's that aroma?" Miranda asked. She paused, searching for the right word. "It's elegant. Sweet, but not sticky."

"Lemon trees," Lucy said dreamily. "Lemons and oranges." They were leaning arm in arm against the back railing, all rules temporarily suspended. "Oh, darling girl, you may drive me wild, but I have to thank you. I never thought I'd ever see anything like this, not in all my life."

The Arcade Street Station was several stops removed from the main depot. On the advice of the railroad agent in Fort Lee, Lucy had booked them through to avoid the confusion of disembarking in a crowd. "Well, honey, we made it!" she said, as they stepped down onto the platform. "And after five straight days of sponge baths, all I can think about is water to my chin and my lavender bath salts. Terra firma, here we come."

Miranda, however, found herself in that curious state midway between elation and deflation that spells journey's end. Parting with Grover had been sad for such a brief acquaintance, but he had promised to look for her at the picture show, and she had sworn to visit the depot "whenever *The Limited* comes in." She was also welcome anytime for a session of five-card draw, this in a whispered aside while Lucy was occupied with the luggage.

Seven o'clock on that particular December evening in Los Angeles could have been June anywhere else. The air was balmy and spiced with the scent of the geraniums climbing the station wall, and the rising moon was the pale gold of midsummer. The other passengers had all departed, and the platform was empty. Lucy had powdered her nose twice and was sitting on her trunk. Miranda walked slowly along the platform, then to the station door to peer into the waiting room, then back along the platform.

"Maybe we should wait out front," she said tentatively.

"I'm not leaving our bags."

At seven-thirty Miranda made her suggestion again. "I am not about to stand on the street corner like some chippie!" was the reply, so she went back to pacing.

At eight o'clock Lucy snapped open her purse and took out C.J.'s telegram. "Auf Wiedersehen and Merry Christmas," she read to herself. "Stop C.J. Now there's a thought." She wadded the flimsy paper into a ball, made a move as if to toss it onto the tracks, then, ever the lady, replaced it in her purse. "Here," she said, handing Miranda a nickel. "Go ask the stationmaster to let you use the telephone."

Miranda returned after only a few minutes. "They're not there."

"You're sure you called the right number?"

"Yes, ma'am," she said uneasily. "It was the Hollywood Hotel, that was what the lady there said." She did not tell Lucy that the switchboard operator had snarled, "I ain't puttin' through any more calls to that deadbeat," before abruptly breaking the connection.

At nine o'clock Lucy rose briefly, ordered Miranda to put on her overcoat, and sat down again with her ankles primly pressed together and an iron grip on her purse. Miranda sat on her suitcase and concentrated on swallowing the panic rising bitter and green up the back of her throat. It was very like The Boss to overlook something as basic as meeting a train. But not the Donnellys...or Bobby. Please, not Bobby.

"Get your hand out of your mouth," Lucy said sharply.

"Yes'm."

"What in heaven's name came over me?" Lucy said, gazing out over the tracks. "Rent the house. Put every stick of furniture into storage. Leave all my friends, farm out my students—oh, and my piano." Her gray eyes brimmed and she moaned, "My beautiful Steinway. Sitting in a crate in that awful warehouse. Alone, unloved, *untuned*." She blinked her tears away impatiently. "Lucy Gaines, you have been a fool."

"They wouldn't forget us, Auntie. Not on Christmas Eve."

Lucy stood, smoothed her skirt down over her hips, folded her arms at her waist, and looked down at Miranda, who was staring up at her helplessly.

"I am going to kill that man," Lucy said. "Assuming he ever shows his face," she added dryly. "And then, my little actress, we are going to get on the next train heading east and...go...home."

Bouquets and Brickbats

The flowers made their entrance first. A bouquet of two dozen red carnations nosed out from behind the station door, waved up and down as if signaling a passing ship, then inched backward. The door closed abruptly, separating a number of blossoms from stems, and Miranda heard whispering and what sounded like smothered laughter.

She looked down the platform—Lucy was carrying on a heated argument with herself and torturing her handkerchief—then over her shoulder. The station door opened a crack. A hand appeared and drummed a casual tattoo. The crack widened. A boy's head drifted lazily into view. Black curls tumbled over the high forehead, green eyes sparkled wickedly beneath heavy brows, and the wide mouth was lifted in a crooked grin.

Miranda felt her cheeks flush, and something tightened in her chest. She sprang to her feet. Bobby shook his head and pressed a forefinger to his lips. He beckoned to her, slid out of sight, and soundlessly closed the door.

"Oh, Auntie?" Miranda called out. "I'm going to the water fountain." She strolled with painful restraint across the platform, pulled open the door, and was yanked into an embrace that smelled of starched linen, Bay Rum, and Sweet Caporal cigarettes. A watch fob was grinding into her cheek, and over her head a resonant voice was crooning, "Oh, Ridiculous Child, you are return-ed unto me."

"Pipe down, Boss," said Bobby. "I saw her first." He pulled her away from C.J., gave her a swift, fierce hug, then shoved her free. "Lucy gunnin' for us?" he said in a low voice.

"She's threatening to go back home," Miranda whispered. "It's going to take more than flowers, even if they are gorgeous."

"Nickel a dozen. They grow here like weeds."

"This is all very interesting," she hissed, "but where *were* you? The train got in hours ago."

"In a meeting," C.J. said, a little too readily. Bobby snorted and C.J. shot him a poisonous look. "Later," Bobby said as he pushed Miranda toward the door. "We're on, Red. The orphan act, in spades."

"You got my wire?"

Bobby widened his eyes and twisted a finger in his hair. "Oh, Mith Loothie," he lisped, "can you ever for-give me for cowwupting Miwanda?"

"Desist!" C.J. snapped, and cuffed the back of his head. Bobby stumbled against Miranda and they fell through the door out onto the platform, giggling hys-terically.

"I'll lead the charge," C.J. said briskly as he stepped over the boy's outstretched legs. "You hold the rear."

He threw back his shoulders, lifted his head, and strode down the platform with arms flung wide. "Lucinda!" he cried. "Moonflower of my heart! I thought this day would never come!"

Lucy whirled around. "You *thought*? I'll have you know—"

C.J. snatched her hand and kissed it, then whipped the mangled bouquet at her with a flourish. "A wee token of my despair," he said, a full measure of syrup in his voice. "I was trapped, Lucinda, trapped in a meeting with two of the dullest men God ever put breath in. Deliver me from bankers! Hearts of stone and minds to match. But here you are, and nothing could be more of a tonic to this weary old showman than your exquisite face. Welcome to California, Lucinda!"

Lucy stared at him. The smile on his round face was broad and genuine, his china-blue eyes as guileless and winning as a baby's. *He does rather look like a baby*, she thought suddenly. *A little bald-headed baby in a fancy suit.*

"Don't you like your posies, Lucinda?"

"For the umpteenth time, it's Lucy. No one but Father ever called me Lucinda. I loathe the name."

C.J. slipped a hand under her arm. "If he made it sound anything less than a benison, then he was, begging your pardon, a cad," he said warmly. He patted her hand and moved her along the platform, as easily as though they were two old friends strolling a garden at dusk. "It's a beautiful name, as befits a beautiful woman. You've changed your hair, I see. Quite fetching."

"Merciful heavens, why does anyone ever listen to you?"

"Because I am the future. Yours and Miranda's. Let that be, my dear. Grab a bag or three. The trunks will keep till the morrow." They had reached the station door, where Bobby and Miranda were having what appeared to be a serious discussion: Bobby's hands were jammed deep into his pockets and Miranda was frowning.

"Robert, deah boy!" C.J. said robustly. "Aren't you going to greet our guest?"

Bobby whispered something to Miranda, then turned, smiling shyly, and offered his hand. "I sure am glad to see you again, Miss Gaines," he said, pumping Lucy's hand. "I think the world of you, and, and... gee, I missed you something awful."

C.J. put an arm around Lucy's waist. "Didn't we all? The world is a dull and drear place when you are not amongst us."

"What is that aroma?" Lucy said. "It's quite pervasive."

"Sage, I expect," C.J. answered. "Grows wild in the hills. Heavenly, isn't it?"

"No-o-o," Lucy said with a faint grin. "It's soap. Soft soap. Gallons of the stuff."

"Time, I see, has not diminished your perspicacity," C.J. said, forcing a chuckle. "Very amusing. Come along, my chickens. Our chariot awaits."

"That ain't all," Bobby muttered.

They stopped at the stationmaster's office to make arrangements for the trunks, then C.J. shepherded them through the empty waiting room and out the street entrance. "Surprise!" he crowed. "Is that a chariot, or is that a chariot?"

A touring car of breathtaking length was parked at the curb, dramatically spotlit under a streetlamp. Not so much as a fleck of dust marred its perfection. The maroon enamel gleamed with the muted fire of garnets, the white canvas canopy was spotless, the brass side lamps were burnished to gold.

"Gracious!" said Lucy. "Where did that come from?"

"Detroit, I believe," C.J. said smoothly. "The bags, deah boy. Side racks, I think."

Miranda stared at the motorcar, then turned to Bobby. He rolled his eyes, took up the suitcases, and began the task of fitting them into the luggage racks on the running boards. C.J. made a great show of handing Lucy and Miranda into the back, pointing out every knob and button until Lucy finally said, "Yes, Charles, the vase is lovely, but at this hour I'm more interested in the engine."

Bobby buckled the last strap and joined C.J. in the front seat. There was a scuffle at the dashboard followed by frantic whispering, and the windscreen wiper arced briefly. More whispering, a muffled "Ouch!", and the engine turned over, cylinders purring liquidly.

This can't really be his, Miranda thought worriedly, remembering C.J.'s previous motorcar, a decrepit old Model T sold for train fare. She ran a hand over the upholstery. Cut velvet? *Oh, crumbs*, she thought. *I hope he didn't steal it*.

"A tad dark for the full effect," C.J. called over his shoulder, "but behold the City of Angels."

They drove down wide avenues flanked with broad sidewalks and modern-looking office buildings and shops, interspersed with islands of greenery and vest-pocket parks. *It's not much like New York,* Miranda thought. *It's clean as a bone—I'll give it that—but it's not nearly as grand, and where is everybody?* The city was as pristine and ordered as a stage before curtain time—and just as bare: the only people on the streets a small crowd in front of a picture theater letting out. After going through a long tunnel (during which C.J. sounded the horn repeatedly, to Miranda's delight and Lucy's annoyance), they bumped over a tangle of rail-road tracks and headed north. A few minutes later C.J. announced: "We're in Hollywood now."

Here the sense of isolation deepened, the street-lamps welcome oases of light in a world of darkness. Miranda rolled down her window but heard only the whirring of cicadas and the rustling of leaves in the pepper trees lining the dusty streets. The houses were set well back behind scrubby lawns spiked with yucca plants. From what Miranda could see by the occasional uncurtained window or porch light, they differed from the pitched-roof, gingerbread-trimmed Victorians of New Jersey. These were bungalows, primarily of stucco or wood, crouched low to the ground behind squat-pillared porches. Architectural differences aside, how-ever, Miranda found her first glimpse of Hollywood oddly—and depressingly—familiar. *Another plain old ordinary neighborhood,* she thought glumly. *Two cents there's even a Hollywood Ladies' Benevolent Society.*

Block after silent block passed by, until they turned onto a four-lane boulevard divided by the streetcar line. And there it was, rising from the street like a White Star liner towering above its slip. Brilliant with light and sharp white stucco, a clutter of balconies and turrets and grass-green awnings and red tile roofs stretched from one end of the block to the other behind a curved drive and a garden flecked with palm trees—the Hollywood Hotel.

Miranda's breath caught in her throat. "Oh, Auntie, look!"

"I'm looking. I'm definitely looking."

"Splendid little pile, eh?" C.J. tossed back.

"It looks," Lucy said in a strangled voice, "like the Brothers Grimm had designed the Alhambra."

"None of that eastern snobbery, now," C.J. chided. "You're in the West now, and the Spaniards were here before us."

A Christmas party was in progress. The drive was choked with motorcars, the overflow parked haphazardly on the lawn. The party had spilled out onto the front steps and the long veranda overlooking the street. Somewhere inside the building a dance orchestra was playing, at blast level, a syncopated quickstep that made Miranda's feet twitch in her shoes. A couple attempting the Castle walk, in double time with the spinning turns, went careening across the lawn and collapsed in helpless laughter across the hood of an open roadster.

"We'll go 'round back," C.J. said.

"Shouldn't we check in?" Lucy asked.

"Tomorrow, tomorrow," he replied airily. "No need to bother the front desk at this ungodly hour."

"Are you sure?" said Lucy. "I've never heard of—"

C.J. jerked up the hand brake and the big automobile rocked to a halt, springs screeching in protest. "Home again, home again," he said heartily. "Leave the bags, I'll send Donnelly down later."

"Oh, forevermore," said Lucy. "I clean forgot the Donnellys. I'm dying to see Mary again. Where are they?"

"Out," C.J. said shortly. "Chop-chop. All ashore that's going ashore." He led them along an arbored walkway to the back of the hotel and stopped at an unmarked door with a small window grille. He made no move to open it, instead gesturing to the iron staircase zigzagging up the side of the building. "Our own private entrance," he said. "Why mix with riffraff unless you absolutely have to, I always say."

Lucy looked at the stairs, then at C.J. "Hmm" was all she said.

"Quite handy, really," said C.J. Bobby took Miranda's hand and held it tightly.

"What manner of rube do you take me for?" Lucy said calmly.

"Why, Lucinda, whatever do you mean?" C.J. said, laughing nervously. "Let's go up to the suite."

"I've seen fire escapes before, Charles. How much do you owe—"

There was a burst of noise and laughter as a group of partygoers came down the hall inside, toward the door. "Action!" C.J. yelled. He grabbed Lucy and pulled her up the stairs, Miranda and Bobby at their heels. Hearts pounding—the carnations went overboard in a crimson shower on the last turn—they raced up the two flights to the top floor. C.J. tore open the fire door, yanked them through, slammed the door shut, and leaned against it with his feet braced into the carpeting.

"That was a close one," Bobby panted. C.J. glared at him, then dropped his head back and closed his eyes.

Lucy was bent double, struggling for breath. She clutched her head and looked up at C.J. "I lost my hat," she gasped. "Drat you, I lost my hat. And my flowers." She slid down the wall until she was sitting on her heels . . . and began to laugh.

C.J. opened his eyes. Miranda and Bobby stared at each other, then at Lucy.

"Mercy," she gasped, and shook her head. "Have mercy. I didn't expect a brass band. Or a red carpet. But this is— I don't know *what* this is. Three hours late, he shows up in the Queen of Romania's motorcar, and now this." She laughed again. "Well, don't stand there like cigar-store Indians, you two. Help me up."

She flapped the dust out of her skirt and smoothed her hair into place, her impromptu toilette observed in baffled silence. "Come along, Charles," she said brightly. "I'm ready for the grand tour."

"Of what?" he said blankly.

"Why, The American Moving Picture Company, of course. The suite, your offices, headquarters, or whatever you call it."

"Sure," C.J. said uneasily. "Sure thing."

"But, Auntie—"

"Yes, dear?" The face Lucy presented to Miranda was a mask of composure, the smile politeness itself.

"Your hat," Miranda improvised. "Don't you want to go back and get your hat?"

"It's not going anywhere," said Lucy. "Charles?"

"What gives?" Bobby whispered to Miranda as they followed them down the hall. "Why ain't she spittin' tacks?"

"I don't know," she whispered back. "It's downright peculiar."

C.J. fingered a key out of his watch pocket, unlocked the door, and paused with his hand on the knob. "Not exactly the Taj Mahal," he said tensely. "Have to keep expenses down. All for the studio, all for the studio."

"Makes perfect sense to me," Lucy said cheerfully.

C.J. peered at her face, which continued to display only composure, then shrugged, opened the door, and stepped to one side.

Lucy stepped into the doorway and once again began to laugh. "A *capacious* apartment? Really, Charles, I must buy you a dictionary. Oh, come over here, Miranda. This you have to see."

It was immediately apparent that Bobby occupied the left side of the room. The narrow bed was neatly made, and his clothes and belongings (of which there were admittedly few) were stowed out of sight. A row of carefully dusted books lined the back of the dresser, two lamps serving as bookends. Pictures of actors clipped from magazines were pinned around the mirror: Miranda recognized William S. Hart and Mae Marsh and Constance Talmadge. The flowered carpet was swept clean up to the invisible line halving the room.

Over the border chaos reigned. C.J.'s bedspread was a landscape of hillocks and valleys, lumpy over

47

shoes and books and Lord only knew what else. Back issues of *Photoplay*, *Moving Picture World*, and *Variety* fanned in slippery stacks from under the bed and fought for space on the nightstand with coffee cups, ashtrays, and the telephone. The telephone stand was under the open window, on it a gas ring with a crusted tin saucepan, spoons, coffee grounds, soda crackers, and a wedge of extremely aged Cheddar. C.J.'s old theatrical trunk was open at the foot of the bed, the contents exploded onto the floor: a dressing gown of faded plum silk, play scripts and notebooks and canceled checks; bits of paper and yellowed clippings unloosed from their scrapbooks; a length of red damask curtain from the Empire Theater in Omaha, Nebraska; and a Mexican War sword in a crumbling leather scabbard.

"So this is the new home of The American," Lucy said gaily. She crossed to the armchair by the window, nonchalantly flipped the newspapers thereon to the floor, and seated herself. She leaned to one side, chin resting on her hand, and crossed her ankles demurely. "I suppose room service is out of the question, considering maid service has been cut off. Weeks ago, by the look of things. Pity. I could use a sandwich."

"Fired the wench," C.J. bluffed. "Didn't want her messing in my papers."

"Oh, Charles, don't embarrass yourself," Lucy said. "Granted, it was twenty years ago, but I did tour vaudeville one summer and I know the dodges. What I don't understand is why you haven't gotten the bum's rush."

"The Donnellys," Bobby blurted. "Sorry, Boss. She might as well know. Jerry's been tending bar," he said to Lucy, "and Mary's been doing mending for the guests. They're working off our bill." He pointed to the connecting door. "Their room's through there. They're downstairs serving at the party, that's why they're not here."

"A slight financial miscalculation," C.J. said, fiddling with his watch chain. "Costs the earth, this hotel, and we—"

"Yes, yes," Lucy interrupted. "All for the studio. There is some money left from *Cupid,* isn't there?"

"Oh, yes," C.J. harrumphed. "Yes indeedy, yes, yes."

Bobby elbowed Miranda and put out a hand with the thumb and forefinger a scant quarter inch apart. "That much," he mouthed.

"You are truly astounding," Lucy said evenly, "but I give you credit for sheer gall. I don't know who's the bigger fool—you for thinking you could bamboozle me across the country or me for letting you do it."

That was too much for the rigid silence Miranda had been maintaining. "Auntie!" she cried. "Why are you acting this way?"

"What way, darling?"

I do not understand this, Miranda thought. *If she'd argue I'd know what to do.* She clenched her fists and glared at Lucy. "For Pete's sake, aren't you mad at him?"

"I might as well be angry with the tide for coming in," Lucy said serenely. "He is what he is. Why shouldn't I be amused? This is all very entertaining. It doesn't make a bit of difference. I told you we weren't staying."

"No!" Miranda's knees began to shake. "Not now,

not now. Not after…but we're here, we're here—" Her voice broke. She burst into tears and covered her face with her hands.

"Tears won't do it this time," Lucy said gently. "And stop scowling at me, Robert. Change your life, you all said, so I did. I was willing to start over again for something real, but this? I'm sorry, but this isn't worth crossing the street for, let alone an entire continent. No, darling, you have a nice visit with your friends, and we'll go back in the morning."

Into a silence punctuated by Miranda's weeping, C.J. started to applaud, slowly and sharply. "Well done, Lucinda," he said sarcastically. "What a happy Christmas this will be. Ebenezer Scrooge could have taken lessons from you. You have overlooked one salient point, however."

"I hope you don't mean my niece's contract," Lucy said dryly. "A contract assumes a company, and I hardly think this debris qualifies."

C.J. stuck his thumbs under his lapels, assumed his Leader-of-Industry stance, and began to pace in front of her. Bobby handed Miranda his handkerchief and muttered, "Places."

"An arguable point of definition," said C.J. There was a devious glint in his eye; his consonants were crisp, his vowels rounded. "A company is no mere assemblage of buildings and equipment. A company is artists with a shared vision, and the drive and the spirit to see that vision through. We've made pictures on a shoestring before, as you well know, and we can do it again. The American Moving Picture Company is not dead—merely resting. But, as I said, an arguable point.

The *un*-arguable point is this: You cannot return to Leewood Heights."

Lucy folded her arms and dug in. "Is that so. Would you be so good as to tell me why?"

C.J. pivoted on his heel and bent down so his eyes were level with hers. "Do so," he said through gritted teeth, "and Madame Duncan and her marauding gang of corseted gossips will have the upper hand till the day you die."

Lucy moaned softly.

"Perhaps a demonstration? Roberto," he said, eyes locked on hers, "give her the Emma."

"Righto," Bobby said happily. "Props! I need props!" He sprinted to his bed, snatched the pillow from under the coverlet, jammed it into his belt, and buttoned his jacket over it. Miranda sprang to the trunk and snatched up the frayed curtain length. She wadded it into a ball and flipped it to Bobby, who caught it one-handed, wrapped it around his shoulders for a shawl, whipped Miranda's hat off her head, and sashayed over to Lucy.

"Oh, good Lord," she snapped. "I am in no mood for playacting."

Bobby folded his hands under his makeshift bosom. "Language, language," he said in a pinched falsetto. "Back so soon, Miss High and Mighty? You and that troublemaking hellion of yours? That brat sets so much as one toe in my yard and I'll have her sent to reform school. *You* certainly can't control her."

Lucy made a shooing motion. "Stop it, stop it."

"Stop what, you ungrateful hussy? I'll thank you to keep a civil tongue in your head." He sniffed horribly,

51

mimicking Emma's alleged martyrdom to allergies, and pursed his lips.

Miranda twisted the handkerchief in her hands, her lips moving in silent prayer: *Get her, Bobby, get her.* C.J. had stepped back and was watching the performance with a grimly satisfied smile. Almost unconsciously, he had squared his hands to frame the scene.

Bobby pressed on. "We'll take you in hand, Lucy, dear. I've called a special prayer meeting just for the saving of your dirty black soul, and I'll visit you each and every day. You'll repent your sinful ways in no time—"

"*Aoowh!*" Lucy groaned. "Go away, you wretched child. I give up."

Miranda let out a shriek. Bobby tossed her hat into the air. It skimmed over Lucy's head and sailed out the open window.

Stunned silence for a moment, then the room erupted in laughter as all the tensions of the day were released. "Let's go for three!" C.J. bellowed, taking a battered homburg from the trunk and sending it into the night.

Lucy rocked back and forth, clutching her waist. "You people are crazy," she gasped, tears oozing from the corners of her eyes.

"Dance with me, Delicious!" C.J. cried, pulling her to her feet. He spun her around the room in a ragged polka, giddy with laughter and speed, Lucy flushed and breathless. Bobby grabbed Miranda and pulled her up onto his bed. They jumped and bounced the bedclothes into a tangle, all the while yelling, "We're *stay*-ing! We're *stay*-ing!"

C.J. deposited Lucy in the armchair with a neat bow, then closed the trunk, sat on the lid, and crossed his legs. He fished his cigarettes from a pocket and offered one to her; she wrinkled her nose with disgust and shook her head. The victory chant on the bed had changed to "Merry Christmas to us, Merry Christmas to us," screamed to the tune of "Happy Birthday." C.J. rasped a match to life on the sole of his shoe, lit a Caporal, and blew a long, lazy plume of smoke at the ceiling.

Lucy caught his eye. "I've been suckered."

"One born every minute," he said graciously. "Lord knows you've got company in this town."

"We'll not depend on you. I'll teach, sew if I have to. If Miranda gets other offers we'll take them."

"Wise woman. You're here for more than The American, anyhow."

"Oh I am, am I."

"Dear lady, we are on the brink of what promises to be the greatest explosion of creative energy and artistry since the Renaissance." He smiled wryly and said, "For once I'm not exaggerating. It's no accident that we're all out here, you know. Griffith, Ince, even that twit Cecil DeMille. It's more than the sunshine. There's something in the air. Art is made when things shift. When the world is falling to bits, people *need* storytellers."

Lucy looked over at Miranda and Bobby, who were running in circles on the bed, stopping every four steps to strike silly poses and scream, "Happy New Year!" Miranda's braid had come undone, her slip rode below her skirt, and her stockings were around her ankles.

53

The expression on her face was so blindingly happy that Lucy's eyes filled.

A chill breeze lifted the curtain behind her and she shivered, for a moment in shadow. Her eyes met C.J.'s, and something close to understanding passed between them. He arched a questioning eyebrow at her.

"A year," Lucy said quietly. "I'll give you one year."

Another Quiet Afternoon

Lucy Browning Gaines was a woman of many admirable qualities, not the least of which were a talent for organization and a devotion to the Yankee work ethic. Here was a woman who had actually *enjoyed* dismantling the contents of an entire house, the ache in her back a willing exchange for the pleasure of ticking box after filled box off her list. "Packing is an art," she had instructed Miranda. "Look at my suitcase. Everything in tissue, then you lay tissue between the layers and the sachets go in the corners, see?" Miranda rolled shoes in embroidered blouses and thought it a lark to have to sit on her bags to close them. A touch of clutter was Bohemian, after all, and Auntie was sometimes too exacting for words. But if Miranda had ever thought to look back over a lifetime of laundered sheets and hot meals and darned stockings, she would have admitted that Lucy was more than her beloved aunt. Lucy was useful.

The morning after their arrival, Lucy set about tidying up The American Moving Picture Company. She settled accounts with the hotel, releasing the

Donnellys from indentured servitude; extracted from C.J. a promissory note with interest calculated and payment schedule attached; leased the sunny double on the second floor she and Miranda had checked into the night before; sent away, with steely charm and two bits for his troubles, the salesman who arrived with the purchase papers for the Cadillac touring car Mr. Tourneur had been test-driving; sent Jerry to the depot for their trunks; wheedled the formidable woman at the front desk into posting a notice advertising her availability as an instructor of the piano, lessons to commence one month hence, location of studio to be announced, leave your name at the desk and Miss Gaines will contact you; telephoned the superintendent of the Los Angeles County School Board at his home to request a list of accredited public and private schools; and persuaded the housekeeper to send a cleaning crew to the Company's suite. All this by noon, by which hour C.J. had taken to calling her—under his breath and behind her back—The Iron Maiden.

Finances settled to where heads could be held erect and the lobby crossed without being poised for flight, The American gathered for luncheon on the back terrace. The warm spell continued, and the hotel had erected canvas umbrellas to shade the tables. Wisteria climbed the white wall behind them; above, the red tile roof glowed in the sun; and beyond lay the inescapable surround of jagged brown hills.

Lucy sighed contentedly and tipped back her chair to let the sun play over her face. "What a morning!" she said. "Never have I worked so hard on Christmas

Day, not even with twenty and the parson to dinner. I must say everyone I spoke to was very cooperative."

"Took them by surprise, no doubt," said Jerry.

"Like Grant took Richmond," was C.J.'s sarcastic comment.

"I'm sorry if I stepped on your toes, Charles," Lucy said graciously. "I never could bear to see things left undone, and honestly, your affairs were—" She paused delicately. "In some disarray."

"Nothing I haven't been saying for weeks," said Mary Donnelly. "Why we let men run this world when they do such a poor job of it! My hat's off to you."

"And a darlin' hat it is," Jerry said stoutly, lifting the brim to plant a kiss on her cheek.

Miranda let her eyes pan slowly around the table, studying the faces framed by sun and flowers and the distant hills. *I must freeze this memory,* she thought, *like a still from a moving picture.*

First there was Jerry, his brogue as musical as remembered, his manner as gentle. Jeremiah Aloysius Donnelly, Irish to the bone, sentimental, hardworking, and loyal beyond all reason. Handsome, too, with his wavy auburn hair and copper-colored mustache. His darlin' Mary was beside him, more than ever like the brown robin in the poem, plump and sweet, with bright eyes and pink cheeks. Mary was neither fooled nor impressed by C.J., but took him, as she once said, not with a grain of salt so much as a whole pillar.

And there he sat, at the head of the table as if by divine right, Charles James Tourneur, visionary and actress-scarred veteran of the Biograph's famed Fourteenth Street studio, the dingy brownstone where

57

magic and no small amount of history had been made. Also, if you chose to believe him, veteran of every touring theatrical troupe since Molière, the top of the bill in vaudeville, the cabarets of Paris, the goldfields of Mexico—and whatever bit of folderol he needed to illustrate a point, talk someone into doing something they didn't want to do, or amuse himself. A *father figure*, thought Miranda with a giggle, *if you wanted a father like the Pied Piper and Mr. Micawber all rolled into one*.

Then came Auntie, relaxed at last and (thank heavens!) smiling. Then Bobby. How to describe Bobby? She could spend the rest of her life trying to solve the puzzle that was Robert Ian Gilmer, and she fully intended to try. Miranda mentally clicked the shutter on the scene and thought: *I am completely happy*.

"We really are together," she said. "I was afraid it wouldn't happen, but here we are. It's the best Christmas present ever." Her eyes sought Bobby's and he returned a cautious smile. Someday she and Bobby would tell Lucy that empty coffers and chaos had been no surprise to Miranda. Someday, but not today... and not soon.

"I've got an idea," said Lucy.

"Brace yourselves," C.J. groaned.

"What say," she went on regardless, "we reserve a table in the dining room for tonight? Roast goose with all the trimmings, a proper Christmas feast." C.J. cleared his throat, and Lucy laughed and said, "You're square now, remember? And it'll be my treat."

"I suppose that means a tie," Bobby said sourly. "Hey!"

"Pardon," Miranda said sweetly. "My foot slipped."

"It'll be a double celebration, like," said Jerry. "Christmas and you and Missy arrivin' together."

"I'll go arrange it," said Lucy, "then I am going to unpack and take the longest bath known to man or woman. Followed by a nap of similar length."

"You're sure now?" said C.J. "You don't maybe want to run down to City Hall and clean up that messy little situation with the Water Board."

"No, Charles," she laughed. "I'm quite done for today, thank you. Coming, darling?"

"Later, please," said Miranda. "Bobby said he'd take me exploring."

"I don't want you bothering the guests or poking in where you're not welcome."

"We're just going to take a walk," Bobby assured her. "Most everything's closed today. What harm could we do?"

"You two?" C.J. snorted. "God help the Huns if you two ever hit France."

Lucy looked at Bobby. "I assume," she said mildly, "you know what will happen if I catch you anywhere near a card game?"

"Yes, ma'am." He scraped back his chair and stage-whispered to Miranda, "Exit left, dead run."

"Run for your life, boy," said C.J.

Lucy flapped her hands at them. "Shoo! Just be back in time to bathe and change for dinner."

They were up and off, Miranda pausing to strike a

pose and cry, "Give me poker or give me death!" before Bobby jerked her out of sight. They strolled down
Hollywood Boulevard, peering into store windows and
chatting aimlessly. The corner druggist was open for
business, and they stopped in the doorway to gaze
longingly at the soda fountain, the glasses and bottles
sparkling against the mirrored wall behind the long
counter. Bobby eloquently turned out his empty pockets and they walked on. A streetcar clanged by, empty
of passengers.

"What did I tell you?" he said. "Nothing to do in
this burg between engagements."

"It is Christmas."

"What's Christmas to an actor? An extra matinee,
that's all." He turned down a side street into the resi-
dential neighborhood they had driven through the
night before. They walked along the sidewalk, stopping every so often to peer over fences at gardens coming early into bloom.

"I adore exploring strange neighborhoods," said
Miranda. "Especially at dusk, when the lights are on
and you can see in the windows."

"Who would've suspected? Voyeurism in one so
young. Tragic."

"Oh, for Pete's sake, I meant bookshelves and pictures on the wall and seeing everything all lit up like a
stage."

"That is only pleasurable if you know that somewhere, close by, is a house waiting for you."

"It's just a game, Bobby. Like playing spy."

"No," he said slowly. "It's a bad feeling, what I'm

60

talking about, but I wouldn't expect you to understand. Your loneliness comes from another direction."

They were alongside a low stone wall, which was planted with a dense hedge of rambler roses that reached above their heads. A few blossoms had popped open in the unseasonable heat, and Miranda stopped to finger one. "Sometimes I wonder if I'll ever understand you," she said wistfully, bending her nose to the light, sweet scent.

"You stew over the darnedest things," he said. "We understand each other fine. We'll just never be alike. You make things happen. Me, I tend to drift."

"Drift? You set out on your own, you get a job with the Biograph, then with the Company. When I think of all the things you've done and the places you've been, I could just die."

"Not much of one for overreacting, are you?" he said, and grinned. He pivoted, stuck his hands in his pockets, and started walking backward. "You should try this, very good for balance. No, Red, it's like this: Most of the time I do what I do because there isn't any choice."

"I keep forgetting that you don't want to be an actor as much as I do."

"Precisely. I was raised up to be one, no one ever asked me, and after a while it was that or starve."

"Well, what could be worse than starving?"

"Plenty," Bobby said darkly. He turned abruptly so he was beside her again, his face shuttered.

Miranda had once thought Bobby's moodiness romantic, his tersely edited anecdotes of a theatrical upbringing exciting. Orphanhood, she had thought, would be a bond between them, but the pleasant security of her childhood was no match for his. Once, and only once, had he spoken the truth of its horrors to her. It was a Dickensian tale of loneliness and abandonment, far beyond Miranda's enthusiastic and clumsy attempts at empathy.

Of his father Bobby knew nothing, not even his name. What he knew, all he had ever known, was the theater. Not the theater of flower-filled carriages, champagne suppers at Delmonico's, and Broadway houses glittering with gaslight, gilt, and plush velvet, but the shabby desperation of third-rate touring companies and fourth-rate hotels. No home, no education, just a wretched migration from town to town with his mother, an actress of little talent and great beauty sliding down the rusty razor of alcoholism into a hazy world of cracked mirrors, unheated dressing rooms, and hangovers. Her death, he said sadly, had freed him. Freed him to make his way to New York, to trudge from theater to theater growing closer to starvation and despair with every "Sorry, nothing today," until finally he had collapsed in the alley behind the Biograph building. There, one Jerry Donnelly, assistant to cameraman Billy Bitzer, had found him—a filthy alley cat of a boy with a battered knapsack, an overcoat stolen from the wardrobe room of a Chicago theater, and thirty-two cents in his pocket.

This wellspring of pain could not remain hidden from the camera and made for performances of magical sensitivity. Off screen was another matter entirely, however, and Miranda had learned to tread lightly.

Teasing would not bring him out of whatever shadowy corner of his past he was in, and pushing shot the bolt across the door. So she simply said, "Oh," and they walked on in silence.

"Summer here's a stinker, I hear," Bobby said after a minute. "Hotter than the fringes. Everything turns brown."

"How interesting," Miranda said awkwardly. "How hot—"

The open motorcar took the corner behind them with a squeal of brakes that split the quiet afternoon like a scream. Bobby yelped and instinctively pulled Miranda away from the curb. He glanced over his shoulder and his face went white. He grabbed her hand and yelled, "*Run!*"

The motorcar had jumped the curb and was following them . . . *on the sidewalk!* The driver was honking the horn, and they heard high-pitched laughter and a voice bellowing, "Gangway, gangway!" And there was another car in the street, coming straight toward them!

They were running now, hand in hand—but where could they go? The rose hedge stretched the length of the block, a minute before a charming old-fashioned conceit, now an impenetrable wall of thorns.

"If we can beat this idiot behind us . . . to the corner . . . we can jump aside," Bobby panted. "Or maybe try for the street . . ."

The automobile in the street accelerated as it passed them, and Miranda saw, out of the corner of her eye, that it was also open-roofed and packed with policemen. Policemen? That couldn't be right. She glanced again and there they were: some six or eight of them, dressed in blue uniforms and domed helmets like the bobbies in her Sherlock Holmes book, all brandishing billy clubs and screaming at the top of their lungs. As they tore by in a blur of waving arms, Bobby yelled, "Now!"—and pulled her out into the street.

They were there for only a few seconds, gasping for breath and gulping down the dust in their throats, when Miranda screeched, "Bobby, *look!*"

The police car had turned around and was roaring straight back down the street!

Bobby looked wildly to one side, then the other. The Mad Driver was even with them now—but by the time he passed by and they could get back to the sidewalk, the policemen would be on them. He wrapped his arms protectively around Miranda. Heads pounding with the roar and stink of the engines, they crouched in the middle of the street, wide-eyed, trembling . . . and trapped.

The Mad Driver rocketed off the sidewalk and veered into the road a hairbreadth ahead of the policemen. A loud jolly voice boomed, "Hop in!" and suddenly there were hands reaching out for them. Miranda kicked and thrashed until she felt the running board under her feet. Bobby landed just in front of her, arms around the big chrome-plated running lamp, feet braced against the fender.

Miranda's arms were over the door, and someone was holding them down. She lifted her head and saw a slightly built girl of perhaps eighteen, with dark eyes ringed with raccoon smears of eye makeup and a Cupid's-bow mouth caked with lip rouge. Her black hair streamed in tangled ringlets from beneath a wide-brimmed hat, and she was laughing and yelling and bouncing up and down in her seat. "Jump in, sardines!" she cried. "Here's your tin!"

"You okay, Red?" Bobby yelled over his shoulder.

"Aces," she screamed back. "Just hang on!" Although the girl had her by the upper arms, Miranda's hands were free, so she pawed around until she found the inside door handle and grabbed it with both hands. The girl understood at once and let loose of Miranda. She clambered up onto the seat, balanced against the windscreen, and stood—then turned and began shaking her fist and screaming insults at the policemen, who were still on their tail and gaining fast.

I'm being kidnapped, thought Miranda. *I'm being kidnapped by maniacs!*

The girl was no longer blocking her view, so Miranda was able to see The Mad Driver clearly for the first time. He was extremely fat, which was emphasized by his curious costume: a faded seersucker suit intended for a much smaller man (only one button fastened over his sizable stomach and the sleeves rode halfway to his elbows), a striped bow tie, and a squashed porkpie hat tied under his chins with a piece of string.

The Mad Driver squeezed the horn bulb. *Ah-ooh-gah! Ah-ooh-gah!* "Got a grip, kiddies?" he yelled. "Let's make those clowns earn their pay!" He jammed the accelerator to the floor, and they tore down the street in a cloud of dust.

"Who are these people?" Miranda shrieked at Bobby.

"How should I know—*aaah!*" The motorcar slewed

around a corner and Bobby's legs shot out from under him, flailing wildly in midair. Miranda quickly stuck out a foot and hooked him in. He scrambled back to safety, panting curses under his breath.

They had turned onto a wide avenue where the houses were larger and set far apart. The Mad Driver pointed to an entrance coming up on the right. Two square stone pillars flanking the driveway were connected by a wrought-iron arch, at the apex of which scrollwork letters grandly proclaimed: ELLESMERE. A broad flat drive of crushed bluestone wound smoothly between manicured lawns to an imposing Tudor-style stone house with diamond-paned windows and a slate roof. Palm trees and yucca plants notwithstanding, the effect was pure English gentry.

"Know this place," The Mad Driver yelled over the noise of the wind and the engine. "Wanted to buy, they wouldn't sell. Shall we?"

"And how!" the girl yelled back. "The snobs."

The Mad Driver pulled hard on the wheel and they fishtailed between the pillars and up the drive, spattering gravel into the flower beds. He braked to a stop under the porte cochere, the engine idling raggedly, and swiveled around to look behind him. "See anything, Mabel?"

The girl looked back toward the road, shading her eyes with her hand. "Nope. We lost 'em."

Bobby unfolded himself slowly and began to climb down from the running board.

"Hey, you!" said Mabel. "Stay put, you're in for the finish now." Bobby was opening his mouth to reply when she shrieked, "Hit the gas, baby, here they come!"

The motorcar jerked back to life and backed crookedly down the drive until The Mad Driver saw the policemen tear under the arch. "Got an idea," he shouted. He gunned the motor, spun onto the lawn, and headed around the side of the house.

"What's happening?" Miranda wailed. "Where are we going?"

"That's good," the man said cheerfully. "Act upset."

"I *am* upset," she screamed, which merely caused The Mad Driver to throw back his head and laugh loudly. Something about him was so good-natured that Miranda began to laugh, too. Whatever else happened, this was no dull afternoon to be suffered with complaints and daydreaming.

They rounded the house, and there lay the glory of Ellesmere. Two full acres of lawns and gardens descended in a graceful sweep from the back of the house in a formally laid-out pattern of terraces and flower beds. There were topiary trees and bushes pruned to replicate animals and chess pieces, flagstone paths and brick walkways, arbors and pergolas and marble fauns. It was an eye-popping display of money and taste and cheap labor.

The focal point was a cement fishpond surrounded with an ornamental stone coping. From its center rose a bronze statue of Diana. This particular Goddess of the Hunt did not hold the traditional bow in her upraised arms, but a scallop-shaped basin from which water dripped delicately to the water lilies at her feet.

The Mad Driver crouched low over the wheel, took a deep breath, and set his course. The motorcar jounced and bumped downward over the flagstone terraces, lurching wildly from side to side. They reached the lowest terrace, the fishpond looming majestically across a short stretch of turf.

"You'll never make it!" Mabel screeched.

"Oh yes he will," Bobby hollered. "Gun it, gun it!" He glanced back, and Miranda saw that he was as excited as she. "Go, go!" she yelled.

The motorcar launched off the terrace, flew over the coping around the pond—and landed foursquare with a hideous jolt as the front bumper hit Diana. A sheet of water billowed up and spilled onto the lawn. The radiator burst with a loud *bang!* and a hissing jet of steam erupted. The radiator cap shot skyward, spinning and winking in the late afternoon sun, then fell gently to earth. Then silence.

At the moment of impact Miranda and Bobby were bounced off into the water. Bobby struggled to his feet and offered his hand to Miranda, who was sitting in the water, staring openmouthed up at the wrecked motorcar. Diana was leaning at an angle over the hood. Her fountain mechanism had survived the collision, and water was spilling from her shell onto The Mad Driver and Mabel—who were taking a pantomime shower bath, rubbing themselves with invisible soap, and screeching with merry abandon.

Miranda stood, water streaming from her clothing. Her hair was plastered in dripping strands across her face. "Who *are* these people?"

Bobby's lopsided grin went ear to ear. "I think I got it figured," he said, eyes sparkling. "You ever heard of— Jeezus beezus, the cops!"

The policemen had opted for ground level, and had reached the pond via a wide pincer movement around the edge of the lawn. They were out of their motorcar and running toward the pond, clubs raised. The first to arrive, a beefy fellow with terrifying eyebrows, clambered over the back of the motorcar and began hitting The Mad Driver and Mabel with his club. Mabel escaped over the windscreen (leaving a piece of her skirt snagged on the wipers) and hid behind Diana, dodging blows and squealing with glee.

Within seconds the pond was filled with policemen, hitting and splashing and sliding and bellowing. One short fellow chased Bobby in circles around the perimeter, the two of them slipping and wallowing through the lily pads.

Miranda had just found a relatively safe perch on the back bumper when she heard, above the din, shouts coming from the direction of the house. A middle-aged man in dinner clothes was bounding down the terraces, taking the steps two and three at a time. A napkin was tucked in his collar and he was waving a drumstick. An elegantly dressed woman and a young boy in a sailor suit were running after him.

The man ran up to the pond, shouting, "Get off my property! Get off my property!" This had absolutely no effect, and his shouts increased in volume and intensity.

The woman ran up and attempted to restrain him, and he threw her off angrily, shouting all the while. "Chester, stop it, please," she pleaded. "You'll have a stroke."

"I don't care!" he bellowed angrily. "I want them gone. Stop it, you hoodlums, stop it! Get out, get—"

A voice rose, brisk and commanding above the chaos, and sounded a single word:

"*Cut.*"

"Cut?" said Miranda. "Oh, for crying out loud."

She turned her head in the direction of the commanding voice—and saw the third motorcar. Another dusty black Model T, but this one had a wooden platform built out over the hood. Bolted to the platform was a hand-cranked camera on a tripod, a wooden-box Pathé like Jerry Donnelly's beloved Baby. The astonishing afternoon of tearaway speed and panicky thrills had been a moving picture!

The action wobbled to a halt. The Keystone Cops exited the pond, slapping each other on the back and chatting amiably, removing their helmets, and shaking water off their uniforms. The Mad Driver descended from the hood with surprising agility and waded to the back of the car.

"There's my little trouper," he said to Miranda. He escorted her down from the bumper over to the wall, holding her lightly by the elbow. "You didn't get hurt, did you?"

"She okay?" Mabel yelled at him. She was standing in the middle of the pond, hat tipped over one eye, wringing out her skirt.

"Well?" the man said, blue eyes twinkling. "Are you?"

"Uh-huh," said Miranda. "I'm fine. Not hurt a bit."

"Glad to hear it. You stay right there, I gotta talk to Rolleigh for a minute. Hey, Mabel," he boomed, "shake a leg . . . it's a figure of speech, you nitwit." He sighed and looked down at Miranda. "She's a cuckoo bird, that one." He smiled at her, shrugged, and slogged across the pond. As he and Mabel strolled arm in arm to the camera car, she turned back to blow a kiss at Miranda.

Miranda sat glumly on the pond wall, chin in hand. Bobby came up and sat beside her. "You didn't guess, did you?" he said, leaning over to shake water from his hair.

"I never even spotted the camera car," she said disgustedly. "Some professional I am."

"You know, those clubs are padded cotton. Don't hurt at all." He lifted his head. "This should be good."

A tall sturdy-looking man was striding briskly toward the pond, megaphone in hand. He was nattily attired in a pinstripe suit, spats, and a straw boater set at a jaunty angle. "Sorry, folks," he called out. "All been a mistake. We lost our way."

But Chester Ellis, Master of Ellesmere, was not about to give up his anger so easily. "Who in hell *are* you?" he bellowed. "And just what do you propose to do about all this?"

"Sennett's the name," the man replied. "Mack Sennett. Sennett Productions." He spoke with a pronounced New York accent, and his smile was infectious, radiating a kind of rough good humor. "Lead car went astray and we had to follow. We'll take care of any damages, no problem."

Chester Ellis stabbed the drumstick at Sennett's face. "If you think you can get away with this kind of shenanigans, you are sadly mis—"

71

"Pop?"

"—sadly mistaken. My lawyer will— What is it, Kevin?"

The boy in the sailor suit was tugging Chester's jacket. His eyes were shining and his cheeks were flushed. "Pop, it's Fatty."

"What?"

"Fatty and Mabel. From the picture show."

"Who?"

"Fatty and *Mabel*. And the Keystone Cops. I told you a million times, they're my *favorite*."

Sennett bent down. "Kevin, is it? Well, Kevin, why don't you go over and introduce yourself to Mr. Arbuckle and Miss Normand. I'm sure they'd love to meet a real fan. I'll bet if you ask real nice, they'll send you an autographed picture. You'd like that, wouldn't you?" The boy grabbed Chester's hand and pulled him away without so much as another word, Mrs. Ellis following with a grateful smile.

Sennett chuckled to himself, then noticed Miranda and Bobby. "Say, you kids okay? No use for amateurs as a rule, but you two roll with the punches a treat."

"Amateurs?" said Miranda. "*We* are with The American Moving Picture Company."

"Never heard of it."

"Be a sport, Mack," Bobby said mildly. "We'll take stunt pay, a fin apiece."

Sennett stared at him, then narrowed his eyes. "Jeezum crow, Fourteenth Street. The kid from the prop room." He snapped his fingers. "Diller? Giller?"

"Gilmer. Robert Gilmer."

"Yeah, Bobby! You ain't still with the Biograph?"

"Nah," said Bobby. "The American, like she said. This is Miranda Gaines. We're out here with C.J.—it's his company. Donnelly's here, too."

"Well, good night, Irene. New York must be empty. Where ya bunked?"

"The Hollywood."

"Charlie's going first-class these days. Come on, I'll drop yez off." He laughed and added, "With yer five-spots. Come out to the studio on Friday and we'll shoot the pickup shots. Can you scream, sweetheart?" he said to Miranda.

"Can I!" she said eagerly. "Like a factory whistle."

"We don't need the sound, just the look. Wear the same clothes—you, too, Gilmer—and don't wash 'em. We'll pay you for the day. And tell Charlie to ring me sometime. The old rascal."

The sun was well behind the hills when Miranda and Bobby returned to the hotel. One of the porch regulars, loud of tie and oily of manner, came tripping down the front steps as they were wearily trudging up them.

"Gilmer," he snickered. "What have you been up to?"

"Working."

An eyebrow went up. "Digging ditches?"

"Sennett," Bobby said blandly. "New Arbuckle picture."

"Too, too exhausting," Miranda said airily, and they sailed up the steps.

They were waiting in the lobby, Lucy tensely toying with the clasp on her purse. She was wearing her

73

new blue net evening dress, with a corsage of tea roses and ferns at her waist. Mary was in garnet velvet, with aigrettes in her hair. C.J. and Jerry had on their best suits and bore evidence of both the barbershop and the shoeshine stand. They turned as one when the door opened.

"Now for the hard part," Bobby muttered.

"Well, she can't drag me back to New Jersey just 'cause I got wet," Miranda whispered. "And we did find work." She lifted her chin, threw open her arms, and cried, "Auntie! You'll never guess what happened!"

No Chinese Dogs
Who Act

One quiet afternoon with the boys of Keystone and Lucy put her stylishly shod foot down: No more hotel living. And no, she did not care if the Hollywood Hotel was, as Miranda wailed, "only the entire center of the film game, that's all." Polite French for a glorified theatrical boardinghouse was more like it.

Especially after what had been planned as a sedate, celebratory Christmas dinner. The story of the madcap afternoon, which Bobby christened Mr. and Miss Toad's Wild Ride, was told and retold until it seemed every waiter was in on the joke. Diners at nearby tables kicked in with their Fatty and Mabel anecdotes. One juicy contribution involving the Bathing Beauties, a bathtub, and a fire hose prompted Lucy to cover Miranda's ears, which only sparked a round of laughter and applause, Miranda rolling her eyes and milking the moment.

The evening was capped by C.J.'s attempt at a famous Roscoe Arbuckle trick perfected in the dining room of the Alexandria Hotel in downtown Los Angeles. You took a starched white linen napkin, folded it into a slingshot, placed a butter pat in the center, grabbed the corners, and snapped the napkin open smartly. The butter flipped to the ceiling and stuck, where, depending on the temperature of the room, it either dropped on an unsuspecting victim or melted into a grease spot. "All my good work come to naught," Lucy muttered angrily, as the Company was politely and firmly ushered out of the dining room by the redoubtable Mrs. Hershey, the hotel manager. Oh, *she* knew all about actors and their shenanigans—there was little you could tell her on *that* score—but damage to the paint was something else entirely!

Miranda assumed the decision to move on rested with Auntie's desire for normal life, which meant a piano in the parlor, pantry shelves groaning with preserves, and Grandmother's Haviland Limoges service for twelve in the breakfront, thank you very much. Bobby judged it Miss Lucy's attempt to control what few aspects of their new life she could, and said nothing. The smallest boats, he reasoned, bear the least rocking.

The following morning Miranda was ordered to the lobby newsstand with a fistful of nickels to purchase copies of all ("And I mean *all*, you hear me?") the Los Angeles daily papers. Lucy pitched camp on her bed with the newspapers, a telephone directory, and an enormous map of the Greater Los Angeles area spread open across the coverlet. Glasses at nose tip, pencil behind ear, she looked for all the world like a harried general planning an invasion. Which, truth be told, she was.

"I'm not looking to rent Buckingham Palace," she said testily. "Two or three bedrooms, a parlor big enough for a piano, and a decent front porch. A sweet little house in a nice neighborhood." She dropped the receiver on the hook with a bang. "Is that asking too much?"

By nightfall she had an angry ring around her ear, the nauseated onset of a sick headache, and a list of rentals that warranted inspection. They would begin the following morning at nine *sharp*, she announced, dressed to make the proper impression. Bobby would accompany them; six weeks in California qualified him as Native Guide.

They gained little that first day but sore feet. Lunch, taken on a park bench downtown, was a frugal repast of oranges (nicked from the gardens behind the hotel) and soda crackers washed down with water from a sidewalk dispenser. A penny in the slot, a grinding of gears and a clunk, and down came a tiny paper cup of ice water. Lucy had to admit this was a touch of civilization of which not even New York could boast, and she treated them all to several cups apiece.

Miranda didn't much care if they ever found a home—riding the fire-engine-red streetcars was paradise. "Even better than the subway," she told Bobby as they rattled through the dusty countryside. "You can watch the orchards go by, like on *The Limited*."

"Just don't try for dinner," he said, pointing out the sign posted on the back wall of the car.

"Passengers are requested not to shoot rabbits from the rear platform," Miranda read out. "Now, that's something you don't see in New York!"

The second day was an eye-opener. Many of the rental ads said NO CHINESE, NO DOGS, and above all, NO MOVIES, the slang term covering all picture people from directors to dress extras. "Do we look like actors?" Lucy asked the owner of a quaint clapboard just off the Edendale line. "And what is so terrible about actors, anyway?" This was his cue for a lengthy harangue on how those lowlifes at the Sennett compound, some five blocks away, had *ruined* what had been a decent neighborhood, what with the noise and the motorcars racing up and down the street and the painted women coming and going at all hours—

"I am not an actor," Lucy interrupted, drawing herself up with pride. "I am a piano teacher."

"Pianos?" the man yelped. "They make more noise than actors!" And he slammed the door in her face.

"That's just a taste of what I've faced all my life," Bobby said to her as they waited on the corner for the streetcar.

"I knew myself, from past experience," she answered. "I thought times had changed."

"Nothing's changed," he said bitterly. "C.J. says it's because civilians are jealous of theatricals—all that footloose and fancy-free guff—but my guess is ignorant people always need a scapegoat. Chinese, Jews, the Irish. Actors."

"And dogs," Miranda added brightly. "Don't forget dogs."

The answer lay not in the wilds of Edendale, nor in

any of the other communities sprouting off the sprawling streetcar system. The answer lay a scant quarter
mile from the hotel, in a block of older dwellings on
Talmadge Street between Fountain and Prospect behind a vast scrubby vacant lot facing the broad diago-
nal slash of Hollywood Boulevard. They found it on
the afternoon of the third day, a dun-colored stucco
bungalow with a deceptive appearance. Unremarkable
from the street, it went long and deep as though a good-
sized house had been placed lengthwise on the lot.

The front porch spanned the width of the house
and was supported by white wooden pillars. Grape ivy
had captured one end, the gnarled vines snaking up a
pillar to wrest the gutter loose. The front door opened
directly onto the spine of the house, a spacious hall
lined with waist-high bookcases. A telephone niche
with a cracked leather seat was beside the front door,
opposite the coat closet. You entered the parlor, on the
right, and the dining room, on the left, through wide
arches.

The kitchen opened off the dining room through a
swinging door and gave onto a cramped pantry with a
stone floor, a tin sink, and a Dutch door to the backyard. This was large and sunny but a study in neglect:
beaten earth and weeds, rusted debris piled against the
weathered property fence, a chewed-looking stand of
eucalyptus, and one magnificent lemon tree.

The center hall formed a T with the back hallway,
which was dismally lit by wall sconces with orange
flame-shaped bulbs. Doors opened onto a linen closet
littered with mouse droppings; the pull-down ladder to
the attic; a bath with chipped white enamel fixtures,

black-and-white octagonal tile flooring, and a large claw-foot tub a previous tenant had painted a vile shade of pink; and three bedrooms shaded to an underwater murkiness by canvas awnings.

The floors throughout were scratched and dull, the doorjambs and light switches grimy with finger marks. The parlor wallpaper hung in filthy shreds from the plaster walls. The kitchen made even Bobby shudder, and the bedrooms had not been dusted since McKinley held office. The rent, however, was extremely reasonable. Suspiciously so.

The landlord, a spare sour-faced man, told them flatly that he didn't care if they were Chinese actors with a trained dog act as long as the rent was paid on time and in cash. He didn't care if Miss Gaines had two pianos and a steam calliope—that was the neighbors' problem, not his. No, he wouldn't paint the place, but if she wanted to, be his guest, just don't expect him to pay for it. He hoped she wasn't an art lover because he didn't like a lot of nail holes in the walls and she should consider herself lucky to find *anything* in this neighborhood, just ask. Why, there was a house on the next block with two tiny bedrooms and no yard to speak of that went for forty dollars a month, which didn't include water, did she know how much water cost—

"I'm sure you have your concerns," Lucy said starchily, snapping open her purse, "as I have mine. I am prepared to take occupancy in one week, provided you give me the keys immediately so I can boil this pigsty. Here is the January rent, twenty-four dollars as advertised. I am withholding eight dollars for the week

I shall spend improving your property. That comes to sixteen dollars. I assume you can give me a receipt?"

Bobby motioned Miranda out onto the front porch. "Look," he said excitedly.

"Where? What are you so—"

He grabbed her shoulders and turned her so she faced west, away from the foothills. "What do you see?"

"The street. The vacant lot, trees, some buildings in the distance."

"Some buildings in the distance," he echoed in her ear. "Three blocks over, Hollywood crosses Sunset."

"So?" she said impatiently.

"The Fine Arts lot, you dummy."

"Griffith," she breathed.

"Miss Lucy's landed you in the catbird seat, and she doesn't even know it."

When they returned to the hotel, Lucy wired the warehouse in Bayonne to have the contents of the Pine Street house shipped by rail. "I don't know where I'm going to put everything," she complained. "I suppose the music room'll take the strain off the parlor—"

"What about all that clobber in the attic?" said Miranda. "The velocipede, Grandfather's trunks."

"They can hold the attic crates for now." She frowned. "Graph paper. I'll get some graph paper and make a floor plan. Fetch me that pad on the desk, darling. I need to make a list of cleaning supplies. Where do you think you're going?" she said to Bobby, who was stealthily making for the door.

"Mere inches from escape," he muttered. "Nowhere, ma'am. Nowhere at all."

"Do you know of a reputable hardware store near here?"

"There's one on the next block. I don't know if it's any good."

"Wait while I write a list, then you and Miranda go get what I want. Three dollars should cover it. Have them deliver to the house, then take the streetcar over and meet them; have them put everything in the kitchen. Here's the front-door key, and a dime to tip the boy. Then come straight back. No lollygagging now, you hear me?"

"Uh-huh. I mean, yes, sir."

"Just you wait," Miranda said to him. They were descending the stairs to the lobby, Miranda with stately grace as she imagined a plumed headdress and a beaded gown trailing behind her. She paused and laid a hand on the railing, then pivoted and leaned her head against the wall. "Your paltry life shall become as one with the Egyptian slaves of old."

"Who are you supposed to be," he snorted, "Theda Bara?"

"I am Mi-*rahn*-dah," she intoned. "Goddess of the Paint Bucket, Empress of the Cleaning Rag. Thou shalt kneel before me, infidel dog."

"Cut it out. I got an idea."

"Chatter on, dog boy."

"You want to listen or audition? I got my fiver from Mack. We can catch a soda at the drugstore on the way back. How's she gonna know when the delivery boy gets there?"

"You're on— Sennett. We're supposed to go out there on Friday. What if she doesn't let us?"

"She can't stop me," he said thoughtfully, "but she might try to stop you. All those stories have her pretty rattled."

"What if we ask her to chaperone?"

"Are you nuts? She'll clean out his office, then tell him how to direct the picture."

"Jerry," she said decisively. "She trusts Jerry; he can chaperone. We'll tell her they can't finish the picture without us. She tries to stop us, it's restraint of trade."

"As the twig is bent," Bobby said with mock despair, "so grows the tree."

Miranda would remember the following week as a blur that stank of paint and ammonia, and left her leaden-footed and light-headed with fatigue. Even the day at Sennett Productions proved poor respite. Mack was nowhere in sight, closeted with the writers in his tower office. She and Bobby stood on the running board of a motorcar positioned by a roaring wind machine and screamed...and screamed...and screamed, while the bored cameraman cranked away and a nameless assistant director cleaned his fingernails with a penknife. They were home by noon.

Bobby's attitude toward housework of any kind, which he considered "girl stuff," improved markedly when Lucy offered him fifty cents for each dawn-to-dusk day of hauling and sweeping and let him dispose of the backyard rubbish with a bonfire. To Miranda's pathetic glances and oblique remarks about slave labor she replied, "You got me here, ducky, the least you can do is scrub a few floors." The Donnellys came over every afternoon when they finished at the hotel (Jerry was still tending bar, claiming it was a better source of gossip than the trade papers) and joined the work with spirit and humor. C.J. was courting potential backers. Or so he claimed whenever he ran into them at day's end—as he was invariably setting forth in a freshly pressed suit, reeking of cologne and evasion.

Finally, the walls were as fresh and white as gallon upon gallon of paint could make them. The hardwood floors gleamed honey-brown as they had not since the day they were laid, reflecting down the hall in the glass bookcase doors Miranda had buffed to an icy sparkle with vinegar water and newspaper wads. Every shelf in every closet was lined with blue-and-white-checked paper, tacked down and edged with a pierced white paper frill Lucy spotted in the hardware store and *had* to have. Gingham curtains billowed at the kitchen windows, the old black range gleamed like anthracite, and the linoleum revealed its original pattern through a fresh coat of paste wax.

On the eve of The Big Move, Lucy again suggested a dining-room feast as reward for all their hard work, and to compensate for all the sandwiches downed on the fly. After dessert was served, the coffee poured, and various waistbands surreptitiously unbuttoned, a questioning look passed between her and Mary.

"Now's as good a time as any," Mary said encouragingly.

"Well, Robert," Lucy said lightly, "are you all packed?"

"Where am I goin'?"

Miranda's heart began to thump.

Lucy took her fork and drew it along the tablecloth, scoring tracks in the linen. "You know, that back bedroom is just going begging, and there's lots of furniture in those crates. A sturdy little mahogany bed that belonged to my brother, bookcases, a desk. I was wondering..."

Bobby's expression was somewhere between longing and apprehension. "I thought you and Mary were going to start a dressmaking business."

"So we are, but there's no reason I can't work out of my bedroom. With the dressing table," she said to Mary, "my cheval mirror, and a screen, I think I can create quite a fashionable atmosphere. Homey, too."

"That's very clever. When you try things on in a shop," Mary mused, "they always look different when you get them home."

"Wait a minute." Bobby glanced at Miranda. "I thought I was a bad influence."

Lucy gazed at him for a moment, then at Miranda, who was blushing furiously. "All the more reason," she said evenly, "to keep an eye on you."

"Jer'?"

"It's a fine idea, lad."

"What about The Boss?"

"Considerin' his present financial state? Be tickled to pay fer smaller digs."

"This was your doing," Bobby said to Miranda.

"I'm as surprised as you are!"

Bobby leaned his elbows on the table and rested his chin on his fists. He squeezed his eyes shut, then sat back and slapped his palms flat on the table. "I'll do it," he announced. "But only if I pay rent."

"I assumed as much," said Lucy. "Three dollars a

week. That includes breakfast and dinner. You get your own lunch, you do your own laundry, and you help with chores."

"Jake with me. I *do* have one condition, however. A certain Miss Sarah Heartburn will *not* follow me around twenty-four hours a day, she will *not* bust in on me in the bathroom or dog me like a puppy—"

"When do I do that?" Miranda said hotly.

"Jeez, only every minute since you met me!"

"For Pete's sake, you make me sound like a three-year-old."

"Hey, if the shoe fits—"

"The two o' yez," Jerry cut in, "would try the patience of a whole calendar of saints. Well, boy, what have you got to say to Miss Gaines?"

"Shake on it?"

"That I will," said Lucy. "We have a deal."

Their bags were packed by nine the next morning. Miranda waited in the lobby while Lucy ran up to the room to make certain not so much as a hairpin had been left behind. The shipment from New Jersey had arrived by rail the day before. Jerry and Bobby would see to loading the rented van, swing by the Hollywood for the trunks, and meet them at the house. C.J. had appropriated the pleasure of escorting "my ladies"—in a taxicab, no less—to their new abode. An honor no doubt based, Miranda decided, on the choice between a few suitcases and a vanful of crates.

She stood by the front desk idly watching the lobby traffic swirl in and out among the potted palms. The actors you could spot a mile off. *Why,* she wondered, *do they always shriek, "Darling!" and fall on each other like long-lost cousins? Stanley and Livingston made less fuss.*

"Looks like an eastern gal," said a low, mournful voice at her elbow. "I ain't got a Chinaman's chance."

The man beside her was staring across the lobby. He was tall and lean, with a hardscrabble toughness to his countenance. He was neatly turned out in a dark suit, a string tie, and beautifully polished western-style boots. There was a slight flush on his lined cheeks, and he was breathing rapidly. Miranda followed his gaze...and saw Lucy, who had just emerged from the elevator with C.J. and the last of their luggage.

Why, forevermore, thought Miranda, *I do believe he's taken a fancy to her.* "I beg your pardon," she said politely. "What was that about eastern gals?"

"They're all so refeened you could die from it," he said, then blinked and looked down at her. The expression in his dark eyes was gentle and a little sad. He whipped off his hat and stood turning it in his hands. His black hair was flecked with gray at the temples and water-combed back from a center part, and there was a ring where his hat had rested. "How do," he said and put out his hand. "Zebulon Calhoun. Zeb to you, Miss."

"Miranda Gaines." *Nice firm grip,* she noticed. "Pleased to meet you. I'm from back East myself. New Jersey, a little town near Fort Lee. Do you know Fort Lee?"

"Yep," he said. "Make Westerns there. Foolish."

"They make Easterns out here."

"Point taken. You in pictures?"

His manner was infectious. "Actress," said Miranda.

"S'posed to meet a feller. Didn't show. You know the folks at this trap?"

"A few," said Miranda, who found herself wishing she had a straw to chew or a split-rail fence to lean against. "Are you by any chance a real cowboy?"

"Was," he said with a smile. "Now I set stunts for Kay-Bee. Bulldoggin', ropin', like that."

Kay-Bee? Quickly, Miranda mentally leafed through six months of *Moving Picture World* magazine. "That's Mr. Ince's studio," she said proudly.

"Inceville, they call it. Fine spread."

"My friend C.J.—he's a director, you know—says he knew Mr. Ince when they worked for Griffith."

"Huh. Everyone in this blame fool town worked for D.W., if you believe 'em. Which I don't."

"Oh, he did. So did my best friend ever in the whole world, Bobby Gilmer, who's an actor. We all made a picture last summer called *Cupid and The Little Sister* and they showed it in New York, on Broadway at the Astor Theatre, with a live orchestra and everything, only they weren't very well rehearsed—"

"You got quite a tongue on you," Zeb said admiringly when she paused for breath. "Can you answer a question?"

"Yep."

"Know that gal over there? The purty little blond?"

"The one yelling at the bald man who just dropped that grip on her foot?" she said, stifling a giggle. C.J. was in rare form, blustering at a bellboy who had come to their aid under the misapprehension that a tip was forthcoming. "That's my aunt Lucy."

"Is she—"

"Married? Nope."

Zeb put his hat on. "Well, come on then. She could use a hand with them bags."

And that was how Zeb came into their lives. Zebulon Amos Calhoun, who was about as dry as a man can get without blowing away. Everything about Zeb was dry: the hard, weather-beaten skin on his homely face; his husky voice; and, above all, his demeanor. When Zeb spoke, the words seemed to trickle from the corner of his mouth, and he would no more have wasted a word than a dollar.

He also possessed more common sense than C.J., which wasn't surprising, and Jerry, which was. This became evident when Lucy's beloved six-foot Steinway was unloaded that afternoon. The crate emerged from the van, a vast shallow wooden affair (the massive round legs had been removed for transport) upended on a dolly, creaking slowly down the ramp with all the perilous dignity of an ocean liner edging into the sea, while the men hauled desperately on ropes to offset the momentum—and Lucy covered her eyes and prayed.

"Please, dear God, not my baby, don't hurt my baby—"

"Easy, boys, easy!" Jerry shouted frantically. There was a screech of wheels and a muffled thump.

"You can look now," said Miranda.

"Oh. Oh, oh my," Lucy gasped, raising her clasped hands to her mouth. "Oh, thank you."

Bobby wiped his perspiring face on his sleeve. "You plan on givin' lessons in the street?"

"The steps," Lucy moaned.

"I say drag the blasted thing into the house and have done with," C.J. muttered crossly.

"I painted those steps," said Miranda. "And I am not going to paint them again."

"Hold the wire, honey," said Zeb. "What's that big crate?"

Miranda consulted her clipboard. "Number twenty-two—the dining-room table."

"Take the lid," Zeb suggested, "and make a ramp. Dolly up the walk—"

Jerry clapped him on the shoulder. "Good man! She'll ease up sweet as jam."

The van was emptied by dusk, and C.J. and Jerry drove off to return it. The disassembled packing crates were stacked in the backyard to await another bonfire, along with a large box into which all the packing paper and excelsior had gone as the crates had been opened and their contents lugged into the house.

A neighbor from down the block had brought over a rhubarb pie, still warm and bubbling with sugary juice. The elderly lady next door, a bright-eyed creature with a cloud of snowy hair bound in a net, had handed Miranda a plate of cheese and crackers over the side fence. "I don't cook," she said crisply, after they exchanged introductions. "But I garden till hell won't have it." She gestured to the impressive flower beds dwarfing her tiny cottage. "Especially this year. The rains came early."

"Gosh, that's really something, Mrs. Norwood," said Miranda, stretching on tiptoe to get a better view. "It must be an enormous amount of work."

"You're not so dumb as you look. You play that piano I saw or is it just for show?"

"It's my aunt Lucy's. She teaches, and she plays like a dream."

"Tell her to play good and loud. Nothing I like more than a little music in the evening. Now scat, I've got weeding to do."

Zeb seemed unwilling to leave. He and Bobby pored over Lucy's graph-paper plan, determined to place the furniture in the appointed rooms by nightfall. The Steinway was on her legs once again, and amazingly in tune after one month in a warehouse, three thousand miles in a freight car, and the roughest assembly of her life. Lucy couldn't resist stroking the lustrous ebony surface every time she passed, cooing and murmuring as to a child. She was on her knees in the parlor, sorting through boxes of sheet music (a sinfully enjoyable pursuit with all that needed doing) when Miranda burst into the room with Zeb and Bobby at her heels.

"Guess what, Auntie?"

"Scarlatti," Lucy said distractedly. "Where the dickens is my Scarlatti?"

"Auntie!"

"Can't you see I'm in the middle of something?"

"Never mind," said Zeb. "We'll ask later."

Lucy sat back on her heels and silently regarded the tall man who stood behind Miranda, eyes shyly on his boots. He certainly was as neighborly as a body could be, and they could not have gotten through the chaotic, exhausting day without him, but she was beginning to wonder . . . Why was he still here and what did he want?

"Ask me what, Mr. Calhoun?"

"I work for the Kay-Bee company, ma'am, in Santa Monica. I thought Miss Miranda and Bob here could come out so I could show 'em 'round, let 'em meet a few of the directors. When you get settled," he said diplomatically. "Mebbe in a week or so."

"Is it a violent environment?"

Zeb looked puzzled.

"I ask," Lucy continued, "because my niece has already been subjected to a rather disastrous experience with Mr. Sennett's players. She is, after all, still a child."

"There's some rough types out there, ma'am, I won't lie to you. Old cowhands, Indians, and the like, but Mr. Ince is a real gent. You wouldn't have to worry 'bout these kids; we'd treat 'em fine."

"You would guarantee their safety?"

"With my last breath."

"Then I suppose," Lucy said slowly, "it's worth a try."

Miranda let out a sigh of relief and grinned at Bobby.

"Would you like to come?" Zeb said to Lucy, his voice rising hopefully.

"I plan on it."

"I'll pick you up. Car ain't much, but it's clean."

"That's very kind, but we couldn't possibly put you out—"

"Excuse me, Zeb," Miranda interrupted. "Auntie, can I see you in the kitchen for a moment? It's *terribly* important."

"Take your time," Zeb called after them.

"Now just where," Lucy said as she closed the kitchen door, "is the fire?"

"*Sshhh*, he'll hear you. You know why he's bein' so persistent?"

"Really, Miranda, what's got into you?"

"He's *sweet* on you."

"Oh dear," Lucy said, and actually blushed. "Oh, mercy me. Well."

"We could get jobs out of this, real jobs, with pay-checks and everything, so could you please be nice to him, Auntie, please?"

Lucy had tied a ragged dish towel turban-fashion over her upswept hair. Now she undid the knot and twitched the towel aside. "Well? Don't stand there gawping," she said to Miranda. She fluffed up her hair with her fingers and began to unfasten her work apron at the shoulders. "Go ask him to stay to dinner. It won't be much, but—" She gazed around the room and bit her lip. "I wonder which barrel the good china's in?"

A Night Out

Miranda had never been an early or willing riser. It seemed every morning of her life began with the sound of Lucy's voice, plaintive at first, then rising to despair, while she buried her head in the cooling welter of rumpled sheets and tried to finish a dream ... or escaped from Paris with the Scarlet Pimpernel ... or died of a nameless, painless malady, pale as marble and twice as lovely, while various school-yard nemeses wept 'round her deathbed—

"Miranda Louise Gaines, I am giving you till the count of three, and then I am coming up there!"

Yawn, stretch, grumble, grumble. "I'm up, for cryin' out loud, I'm *up*."

Now Miranda leaped from her bed at first light, ran to the windows, and fumbled through the net lace curtains (it was like throwing feathers) to undo the catch, push open the casement, and gaze out on ... it didn't matter. The palm trees at the end of the block, looking for all the world like the label on a can of Kadota figs; the eucalyptus trees in the backyard, a massed froth of olive-colored plumes stirring in the dawn breeze; the tall bayonets of Mrs. Norwood's yucca (Our Lord's Candles, she called them) rising grandly over the side fence; the bronze-gray silhouette of the mountains.

It was a world as ripe with promise as a blank copybook, as fresh as a newly plowed field. The big red Pacific Electric streetcars were waiting to take her and Bobby anywhere, the foothills and canyons were waiting for them to pack a picnic and go exploring. Sennett was not waiting—unless she wanted to watch Lucy fizz up like a shaken bottle of root beer—but maybe, oh just maybe, there was Kay-Bee waiting or Fine Arts or whatever grandiose scheme Charles James Tourneur had up his French-cuffed sleeve.

What had not been addressed, however, was what Miranda had been referring to in her mind as "dratted old school." She admitted the need for education—ignorance would have hurt her pride if nothing else—but how was she supposed to be the new queen of the cinema if she spent every day in a school just like the one she'd left behind in Leewood Heights?

Bobby came up with the solution. Weren't there home-study courses, he asked Lucy one evening, for children who were invalids? There were—why ask? Miranda remembered, suddenly and uneasily, Gussie Trinchlove, who had vanished from the third grade to be tutored by her mother while she recovered from something called galloping consumption. Silly little Gussie, with her yellow curls and piercing giggle. She had died that May, and the entire class had gone to

95

her funeral, carrying armfuls of lilacs to bank her piteously tiny coffin. Surreptitiously, Miranda felt her own forehead: cool and dry. Where was Bobby headed?

And did Miss Lucy know the superintendent of schools back in Leewood Heights? Indeed, she did. She had taught his daughter Adelina piano for three years and could offer several gray hairs as proof—

"Why, you clever boy!" Lucy exclaimed. "Why didn't I think of it? I could've made the arrangements before we left. I'll write directly and request the materials."

"It made sense the more I thought about it," Bobby said. "Home study, that is."

"We'll start as soon as the lesson plans arrive. I can give the exams. And *you* can help Miranda study," she said dryly. "From what I've observed, your education has a few gaps as well."

This was perfect! Bobby was a genius. She could stay clear of classrooms, tote her schoolbooks around to— *Oh, rats.* "Aunt Lucy?" Miranda said tentatively. "I don't have my schoolbooks. They'll have to send another set."

"I paid good money for those books, Miranda. What in heaven's name did you do with them?"

The final expedition to the banks of the mighty Matawan had been Tommy Stowing's idea, to mark the departure of Miranda Gaines, Founder and now President Emeritus of The Pine Street Irregulars. On the blissful day that had been Miranda's last at Millard Fillmore Middle School (the Irregulars called it Dullard Boremore, which they thought the screaming height of wit), she had rendezvoused with Tommy and

Jimmy after the final bell. They raced home, yelling and shoving each other into snowbanks along the way, filched cookies and matches from Pearl Stowing's pantry, then slid down the icy path to the river and Fort Conan Doyle, a shack the boys had cobbled together from cast-off lumber and odd bits. The roof had fallen in, and the fire they made to warm themselves—and to spice the occasion with the forbidden—was fueled by Miranda's schoolbooks, gleefully fed to the sputtering flames with cries of "Farewell, civics!" "Adieu, French!" "Get lost, Latin!"

"Don't know where they are, Auntie," Miranda said, her smile warmed by memory. "Lost 'em, I expect."

January came to a close in the kind of domestic tranquillity Miranda would have thought impossible a month before. Mary and Lucy were building their dressmaking business through word of mouth and the notices Miranda and Bobby had spent an afternoon lettering for Jerry to post around the hotel. Once again, like slipping into a well-worn cardigan, Miranda had become accustomed to the parade of strangers in and out of her home: women chattering over cups of tea, fabric swatches, and the latest issue of *The Delineator* in the parlor; children knocking on the front door, clutching music in their hot fists, and stumbling awkwardly through scales and "Country Garden" in the parlor; and the ironclad rules of Stay out of the parlor, Stay out of the front hall, Don't speak unless you're spoken to, Be quiet, Be Quiet, BE QUIET.

On Saturdays Lucy taught until noon while Bobby and Miranda did chores. Bobby mowed the lawn, emptied the ashes and black-leaded the stove, swept the front walk, and chopped wood for the coming week. Miranda dusted, dusted, dusted, ran the sweeper over the parlor and dining-room carpets, and mopped the kitchen floor—a task she hated like poison, always left till last, and sometimes cajoled Bobby into doing. When the front door closed behind the last student, the three of them headed for the kitchen. Bobby got the cookie jar, Miranda got the recipe books, Lucy made a pot of cocoa, and they would huddle around the big pine table to plan the menu for supper. "I don't know why we bother," Miranda would say through a mouthful of gingersnaps. "We always have stew and pie. Beef stew, rabbit stew, apple pie, lemon pie. Stew, pie, stew, pie."

The Donnellys came for dinner every Saturday night, as did C.J., who had moved into a closet-sized room on the first floor of the hotel. No matter, said he. The vine-shaded porches tucked about the Hollywood like raisins in a pudding were far more suited to his purpose—convincing some monied individual that what the world needed was a fully funded and immediately operational American Moving Picture Company.

Zeb also became a regular, showing up on the dot of six every Saturday with "a bunch of posies" for the hostess and the latest Victrola records. Zeb was crazy to dance. He had taken mail-order courses for years, practicing in bunkhouses and boardinghouse parlors, impervious to snickers and rude comments as he solemnly placed his feet in the printed footsteps on the paper charts that came with the six easy lessons, carefully stepping around the room with a broom and eventually graduating to actual women whenever he screwed up the nerve to enter a dance parlor. He was surprisingly light on his feet, and he knew how to partner with the slightest pressure on a shoulder, a hand, the small of the back. He worshiped Vernon and Irene Castle, the popular young ballroom team, and knew all their signature dances: the Castle fox-trot, the Castle walk, the one-step, the two-step, and a fiendishly intricate tango.

On the last Saturday in January, Zeb telephoned Miranda to tell her that he'd finally found the right moment to speak to Thomas Ince. She and Bobby had a chance at extra work and he'd even put in a word on C.J.'s behalf. She wasn't to say anything, however, and he'd see her that night. Roses for Miss Lucy this time, and a new record to try out the maxixe.

Miranda kept peeking out the dining-room window while she was setting the table. As soon as she spotted Zeb's Ford come chuffing up the street, she slapped down the rest of the forks and ran to meet him at the front gate.

"You're an awfully nice man," she said, stretching up to kiss his cheek.

"What was that for?" said Zeb. "Not that I mind."

"You know what for. You got us all jobs!"

"Now, honey, don't jump that fence," he said, shaking his head. "You still got to pass muster. Mr. Ince can always use a few more good players, but directors is differnt. They're a dicey lot." He ran a hand over his chin. "So mebbe C.J. shouldn't know—"

"—that this was your idea," Miranda finished. "We'll let him think his old friend heard he was out here and just couldn't live without him. Besides, he'll be wonderful."

"Nothin's set, so keep mum," said Zeb, and pushed open the gate.

"Can I tell Bobby?"

"Go on. You will anyway."

And I'll just bet, thought Miranda as they walked up to the house, *that this doesn't have a diddlebusted thing to do with me or Bobby or C.J. at all. You did it so you could see more of Aunt Lucy.*

After the dinner dishes were dried and put away, they would adjourn to the parlor and light the fire. Jerry would pull out his pipe, Mary would snuggle into her favorite corner of the big velvet davenport with her tatting, and Lucy would stand in the curve of the Steinway, aimlessly tidying stacks of music or fiddling with the tassels on the piano shawl. This was Miranda's cue to suggest, oh so casually, that perhaps Lucy would play a little something? As if she needed coaxing! Sentimental ballads and Irish tunes for the Donnellys, ragtime for Bobby and Zeb, and at least one crash-banger for C.J., who had what Lucy considered an unhealthy appetite for Wagner. Miranda just liked anything she knew the words to. Sometimes they achieved true four-part harmony, Lucy leading with her clear sweet soprano and the others gamely following: Bobby a light tenor, Jerry a bass-baritone, and Miranda an enthusiastic alto.

"You're giving me nerve damage," Bobby complained that evening, after an emotional rendition of "Love's Old Sweet Song."

"I can't help it," Miranda said, averting her head to wipe her eyes on her sleeve. "It's my favorite song in the whole world."

"Mine, too," said a voice under the side window.

"What was that?" said Lucy.

Miranda put a finger to her lips and pointed toward the front hall. "Stay here," she whispered.

Quietly, she opened the front door, tiptoed the length of the porch, and peered around the side of the house. "Mrs. Norwood?"

"You've got caterpillars on your camellias," came the reply. "Just pickin' 'em off. They eat holes in the leaves, you know."

"Would you like to come in? We're going to have coffee and pie."

"What kind?"

"Lemon."

Mrs. Norwood poked her head around the corner of the house. "With meringue?"

"Four inches high."

"I warn you," she said as she trotted across the yard, "I'm a fierce judge of lemon pie. Haven't et a decent one since my ma passed, and that was in '83."

The front gate banged open. "I got them!" a voice bellowed. "By all that's holy, I got them!"

C.J. came striding up the walk, his face flushed with excitement. He was waving a small white envelope.

"Where have you been?" Miranda said with exasperation. "You missed dinner."

"Dinner?" he crowed. "What's a mere meal compared to food for the immortal soul?"

Mrs. Norwood ran up onto the porch. "Miz Gaines?" she called out. "There's some lunatic in your yard."

Lucy's serene voice floated out. "He's no lunatic, dear, he's a director."

"What," Miranda said to C.J., "are you talking about? Quit that!" He was passing the envelope back and forth under her nose like smelling salts.

Lucy and Zeb appeared at the front door.

"Open it, Rat Girl," C.J. chuckled, and handed her the envelope.

Miranda ran a finger under the flap and pulled out six rectangles of colored pasteboard. "Tickets?"

"'Tickets,' she says. Gold and frankincense, child! Passports to Elysium!"

Miranda held one up to the light. "Auditorium of Clune's Theater Beautiful, Fifth and Olive Streets," she read out. "February eighth, eight P.M. *The Clansman*."

Bobby wriggled between Lucy and Zeb. "Hot diggety! He got the ducats!"

"The new Griffith picture?" said Miranda. "We're going to the *premiere*?" She thumbed through the tickets. "Only six?"

"You, me, Mama-San, the Donnellys, and Roberto," C.J. said smugly.

"What about Zeb?"

C.J. struck his forehead with his palm. "I never— I'm sorry, Calhoun. It won't be easy, but maybe I can get another—"

"That's all right," Zeb said kindly. "I've had mine for weeks."

———

102

The crowd in front of Clune's Auditorium on the night of February 8, 1915, spilled off the sidewalk and into the street, the police attempting vainly to keep a path cleared for arriving dignitaries. Scalpers hawking gallery tickets at twice the orchestra rate shouldered through the throng and huddled in odd corners doing last-minute deals with picturegoers who had simply showed up hoping for a chance at a seat, standing room, anything just to get inside the theater. Jaded reporters with press cards in their hatbands squinted through cigarette smoke and smirked knowingly at each other. The Old Man had bummed around the city room all last summer, passing the hat for the scratch to finish this epic—how good could it be? Old hands at the picture game gossiped and shook their heads. Six months to cut a picture? And it was twelve reels, or so they'd heard. Did D.W. actually believe the American public was going to sit and watch one moving picture for *three hours*? He's lost it, they said, nodding sagely. Lost his mind.

The members of the once and future American Moving Picture Company, however, were simply excited to be there, dressed in their best and expecting the best. C.J.'s string pulling and palm greasing had paid off handsomely: Their seats were some twenty rows back, dead center, with a clear view of the screen. The house was packed to the last seat of the top gallery, the crowd chattering with anticipation. The sense of being present at something momentous, or at the very least memorable, charged the air like electricity.

Lucy leaned across Bobby and tapped Miranda on

the knee. "Look," she said, pointing. The door under the proscenium apron opened and the orchestra began filing into the pit. On they came, until Miranda lost count. Dozens of violins, violas, cellos, double basses, enough brass and woodwinds for a marching band, kettledrums like gleaming copper cauldrons, banjos and fifes and strange-looking noisemakers. Off to one side, the organist was setting stops on the console of the massive pipe organ built into the walls of the theater. A whisper sped through the audience like flame through brush. The entire Los Angeles Symphony Orchestra had been hired to play the picture!

The oboe sounded a single plaintive note. The musicians began tuning up, a tuneless mélange of discordant noise, trumpets testing high notes, winds fluting up and down scales, a last energy-releasing blast before getting down to the serious discipline of making music. A side door opened and Joseph Carl Breil, the composer of the score, walked to the podium.

The lights dimmed. A tense silence fell over the crowd.

"Here we go," Bobby said with a catch in his voice.

"Snag number one," C.J. muttered as the main title appeared over the closed curtain, a faint flickering of letters against the dark folds.

"No, no, it's deliberate," Lucy whispered. "It must be."

Breil raised his baton and held it poised for an interminable moment. Like an arrow going into the gold, the baton slashed downward and a mighty fanfare burst forth as the orchestra and organ joined on one fortissimo chord. Miranda felt herself being pressed against the back of her seat as though by a large, insistent hand. The floor was trembling beneath her feet, and for a moment she could not breathe.

"Great balls of fire!" C.J. cried. "What was that!"

The curtain parted slowly over the main title. The stunned audience recovered its wits and began to applaud. The applause grew until it was a rumbling avalanche of resonance, caroming off the walls, building to a rousing pitch of excitement. And the picture began.

Miranda had seen dailies on a painted wall in a makeshift projection room and been amazed. She had even, on one disastrous occasion, witnessed the full-blown beauty of a subtly tinted moving picture in a New York theater and gone on the common journey of awe and wonderment audiences share when the magic is working. But now, as the story of the Camerons and the Stonemans, the story of one half of the country pitted against the other half in tragic struggle, unfolded reel upon reel into the darkened hush of the theater, she began to feel that she had never truly seen a moving picture before.

She could not feel her hands or her feet or the prickly plush seat beneath her. She was weightless, drawn into the screen, soaring up and through a star-filled window as though touched by the hand of Peter Pan. The same instinct that had guided her to a moment of revelation beneath the vast night sky above *The Limited* sounded within her, a small still voice repeating: *Remember this, remember this.*

The images broke over her in bittersweet waves, sadness mingling with joy, grief and horror set against heart-lifting beauty. The telling moments, the sweetness in the details . . . the nostalgic scenes of plantation life, made real by the simplicity of the performances . . . the lovers at twilight, backlit with luminous coronas of gold . . . the bravery of men marching off to battle and the bravery of the women who watched them go. The funny little sentry, sighing wistfully at Elsie Stoneman, and the laughter that ran through the audience like spilled mercury. The Little Colonel's spine-tingling charge across the open battlefield to thrust the ragged Stars and Bars into the very mouth of the cannon. Oh! the thrill of it—and then the aftermath. Miranda bit her lip and clutched herself, rocking back and forth in horror as the camera panned over the battlefield dead, their sightless eyes lifted to the smoke-shrouded sky, twisted as they had fallen, hands frozen to their rifles. The theater was vibrating with sorrow, women weeping openly, some rigid with shock, and over the mournful cry of the cellos rose the sound of grown men sobbing like children.

Miranda was not aware that when John Wilkes Booth crept into Abraham Lincoln's box like a silky black wind she cried out sharply; nor was she aware that when he leaped to the stage of Ford's Theater, leaving behind the mortally wounded president, she yelled, "Stop him, he's getting away!" Bobby's hand was hot over hers as they gripped the shared armrest, beads of perspiration coursing from his temples to wilt his collar. She was not even aware, until the lights came up for the intermission and she looked down at the hand in her lap, that she had chewed her fingernails to the quick and one was bleeding.

She and Bobby could not speak, so they silently wedged themselves into the crowd trudging up the aisles to the auditorium doors. Miranda was light-headed, faintly sick to her stomach, and supremely happy.

The noise in the lobby was deafening. They overheard one man say importantly, "We might as well go home now."

"I'd like to know what for," said his companion.

"You can't shoot all your marbles in the first half and have anything left for the finish," he responded.

"I'll say!" contributed a richly dressed gentleman with a red face. "That battle was a lulu, best I've ever seen, and that assassination was a knockout, but what's he gonna do for a topper? This thing is gonna fizzle out like a wet firecracker—"

"Come on," Bobby said disgustedly, pulling her away. "We don't need to hear this tripe."

"Look, oh my gosh, look, Bobby, look!" Miranda gabbled, her mental fog lifting instantly. "It's Lillian Gish!" She stared across the lobby, hungrily taking in the delicate heart-shaped face, the large gray-blue eyes, the slight build, and the slender, expressive hands. "Oh, she's lovely. I thought Dulcie was the prettiest girl I ever saw, but she's— It's like she's not from this earth." She tugged his sleeve. "Let's go say hello."

"Are you cracked?" He grabbed the back of her blouse. "Come back here!"

Miranda turned around. "I thought you knew her."

He scowled at her and didn't answer.

"You said you worked with her," she persisted.

"I brought her a sandwich once," he muttered savagely.

The tiny blond woman in the feathered hat and the blue dress had noticed them staring and gesturing and began threading her way through the crowd.

"Now look what you've done," Bobby hissed.

Lillian Gish cocked her head inquisitively and looked up at him. "I know you," she said. "Don't I?"

Bobby was blushing furiously. "Yes, ma'am. I used to work at Fourteenth Street. In the prop room."

"Of course!" she said delightedly. "I thought I remembered your face. My sister and I always said you looked enough like Bobby Harron to be his double. The two Bobbys, we used to say."

Miranda's eyes were growing rounder and rounder with every word.

"Are you enjoying the picture?" asked Miss Gish.

"It's the best thing I ever saw in my entire life," Miranda blurted.

She laughed and said, "We can only hope the critics will be so kind. Are you an actress?"

"I think so, I mean, I hope so, I mean, I just hope one day I can be as good as you—" Miranda stopped, feeling her face redden with embarrassment.

"Then work very hard and pay attention," said the actress. She leaned over and whispered in Miranda's ear, "Hard work, that's the secret."

A bell chimed. Intermission was over.

Lillian Gish smiled at the two of them. "It was good to see you again . . . Bobby? Is that right?"

"Yes, ma'am," he said diffidently. "Bobby. This is Miranda."

"Enjoy the rest of the picture, Bobby and Miranda." She fluttered a hand at them and walked away, then turned back and said, "I'm only twenty-one, you know. You don't have to call me ma'am!"

The second half of the picture dealt with Reconstruction, the Confederates brought to hunger and poverty, ground between the battered remains of their pride and the machinations of the evil Congressman Stoneman, who, Miranda guessed from history class, was probably based on Thaddeus Stevens. The finale was pure tent-show melodrama. No finesse, no artistic lighting, just a flat-out cavalry charge to save dear fragile Miss Gish from a bunch of nasty old dirty-minded Yankees. And it worked. The audience screamed and hollered and pounded the floor, one grizzled veteran in the row behind Miranda waving a moth-eaten forage cap and croaking, "Give 'em hell!" Rusty imitations of the fearsome rebel yell, which had not passed those throats for some fifty years except at regimental reunions, split the air. The orchestra swept into a furious rendition of "The Ride of the Valkyries"—and every member of the audience was up on those horses along with the actors, pumping the reins, digging in their spurs, urging them onward to glory.

All, it seemed, but one. Lucy Gaines sat rigid and white-faced, lips compressed, high on her cheeks the flushed patches denoting anger. This Miranda registered in one swift glance, then returned her attention to the screen and thought no more of it until the picture ended and, exhausted and exhilarated, they were on their way home.

The streetcars were jammed to the rails and they

had to wait for half an hour, but finally one came along and they were able to squeeze into the bench on the rear platform.

The impassioned postmortem continued, Jerry and Bobby and Miranda verbally tumbling and spinning, stepping on each other's lines in their eagerness to share opinions and impressions. What did he mean by this; how did he ever think of that! Two remained silent, however: C.J., head in hand on knee in his Rodin pose, and Lucy.

"Didn't you love Mae Marsh the most?" Miranda chattered. "That scene where she dips cotton in soot to make ermine for her dress, for The Little Colonel's homecoming?"

"That was so beautiful," Mary said emotionally, dabbing her eyes with her sodden handkerchief. "The mother's arms reaching out from the doorway—"

"Genius!" Jerry declared. "Any other director would have showed the whole blessed thing. The mother's arms said it all."

"I like the way Griffith came onstage when it was over and just stood there," Bobby said. "No big fanfare, just 'Here I am, that's my picture.'"

Miranda, who was standing at the rail with Bobby, turned to Lucy and said, "Well, Auntie? What did you think?"

"I thought it was dangerous," she replied. "Terribly dangerous."

"What? It was beautiful, it was— It made me want to scream and cry all at once. It was the *best*."

"Don't misunderstand me, darling. I've no wish to insult your precious Griffith. The first half . . . well, yes, it was grand and moving, altogether heartbreaking. I suppose if Mathew Brady'd had a moving picture camera, that's what the Civil War would've looked like. But the rest of it! He's asking for trouble," she said, shaking her head. "Starting with the awful way he depicts the Negro people."

Miranda was interested now. "You mean that stinker who chased The Little Sister over the cliff?"

"It struck me, as the picture went on," said Lucy, "that the Negroes were shown as either slaves or villains. Does that seem fair to you? How do you think your friend Grover would like that?"

"Not very much," Miranda said uneasily.

"Yes. It's something to think about. And that ending! Dear Lord above, what was he thinking with that ending—"

"You mean the Klan riding to save Lillian?" Bobby interrupted. "That was the most thrilling thing I've ever seen. I practically jumped out of my seat!"

"You did," Miranda giggled. "I thought the man behind us was going to bean you."

Bobby slapped her hand away. "Go on, Miss Lucy. *I'm* listening."

"How can I make you understand?" she said. "It *was* thrilling. But I heard stories about the Klan when I was a girl. And plenty from your mama, darling," she said. She motioned for Mary to scoot over, then reached out to Miranda and drew her down beside her. "Her people were Georgia people, you know." Miranda nodded. "Most of them were in the war, one way or another. It wasn't something you could avoid, not in the South. Her father—that would be your grandfather

Thomas—was wounded twice, I think she said once at Chickamauga."

Lucy leaned her head against Miranda's and gazed out at the night. "That war was more terrible than any moving picture could depict," she said softly, "even one as ambitious as *The Clansman*."

She fell silent. The noise around them seemed to diminish until the streetcar was a hushed island of light rattling through empty streets. They waited, each in their own thoughts, Miranda trying to insert the grim daguerreotype countenance of her grandfather into the more dramatic scenes of the picture. Minutes ticked by before Lucy took up the thread, her eyes clouded with remembrance. "War does something to people I can't explain," she said slowly. "I doubt anyone could, unless they'd lived through it. I do know my father was livid on the subject. It wasn't all that long ago, remember; resentments stayed fresh. And your poor mama. Papa wouldn't have her in the house."

"Why?" Miranda asked. "What did she do?"

"She didn't do anything, she was a perfect dear. He just never forgave your father for marrying a southern girl. And her folks were none too pleased she'd married a da—a Yankee."

I never knew, thought Miranda. *It's so divinely tragic, like the Montagues and the Capulets.* She nestled into Lucy's shoulder and whispered, "Tell me how they met."

"I've told you the story a hundred times."

"I know," she said dreamily. "I like to hear it."

"I didn't mean to go off like that," said Lucy. She sat up and blinked rapidly. "Anyway," she said, "Martha knew all about the Klan, being raised down there.

112

Maybe their intentions were noble at first, protecting the womenfolk, or so they claimed, but they were vigilantes. Vigilantes," she repeated firmly. "Lawless, wild, and bigoted."

"Was Grandfather Thomas in the Klan? Like The Little Colonel in the picture?"

"No, thank heavens. He may have been a hothead, but he was no fool."

"In other words," Bobby said, "you don't think those men should be matinee idols, that it's bad business to make them heroes."

"They should not be glorified," Lucy said sternly. "Nor should their deeds be made glorious."

"You're right, Miss Lucy. That is dangerous."

"But it was only a picture," said Miranda.

C.J. lifted his head for the first time.

"Yes, it was," Lucy said gently. "But there's enough truth in it to make you think it's *real* history. I'm afraid folks'll be so carried away—"

C.J. spoke: "*Only a picture?*"

They all turned.

"Only a picture?" he repeated. "It's the End. The end of the picture game. He killed it in one master stroke."

"Come again, Boss?" said Jerry.

"Griffith. He's killed us all. Took every extra in town and the sweetest cast ever assembled and killed us dead. You. Me. All of us. We're finished."

"What are you talking about?" Bobby said. "That was probably the best moving picture ever made."

"Probably?" said C.J., his voice cracking. "The politics don't matter: The art matters. Who can top it?

Hell, who can match it? David himself can't do better—he's killed himself as well. You don't see it, do you, any of you? You go from day to day thinking you're a painter and then bang! Michelangelo. Bloody Michelangelo. God in heaven, boy, what do we do now?"

There was a pause, then Bobby said, quite calmly: "Make better pictures?"

C.J. glared at him, long and hard, then dropped his head to his hands. He did not address them again for the rest of the journey but was heard to mutter from time to time, "Curse the man, curse him to the skies. We're dust. Dust beneath his feet. I am a worm. I am a *worm*." When the streetcar stopped at the hotel, he swung down the stairs and into the night in morose silence, chipping off an icy farewell. The Donnellys followed: Jerry pantomiming despair and strangulation behind his back; Mary pursing her lips with disapproval.

Lucy went into the house immediately upon arrival, claiming fatigue and tight shoes. Although a chill wind from the hills seemed to pierce right through their coats, Miranda and Bobby lingered under the streetlamp, too full of the evening to let go.

"Some story," said Bobby. "Maybe I should call you Reb instead of Red."

"I've only ever gotten pieces," Miranda said. "I do know Mama and Papa didn't come back home to live until after Grandfather died. I'm glad I never knew him. He must have been one mean old man."

"Bet you could've gotten the scoop from Old Lady Duncan," Bobby teased. "Gory details and all."

"Ugh," she said, and shuddered. "No, thank you. Say, what gives with The Boss? I thought he'd be

114

jumping up and down after tonight, yelling about art and camera angles. He's always going on about how they started together, him and Mr. Griffith, and how they make the same sort of pictures."

"Oh, they're cut from the same cloth. Worked with 'em both, I should know. And C.J. is a born director—" He cast about for the right words. "I see it this way. Griffith's Broadway; C.J.'s the road company. Nothing wrong with that, but for all his talk he'll never be the genius Griffith is. It's what drives him. If you want to be dramatic—and you usually do—it's his demon."

"I think he's brave," Miranda said stoutly.

"How do you figure that?"

"Well, if everyone knows Griffith's the best and they keep at it anyway . . . don't you think that's brave?"

"I'd keep that bit of insight to myself was I you."

"As if you had to ask."

The parlor went dark, leaving only the dim glow from the porch light. "Standing in the middle of the street till all hours," Bobby said. "Lucy Goosie'll take a switch to us."

They opened the gate and went up the walk. Miranda let out a long breath and stopped.

"What now?" said Bobby.

"'Make better pictures,'" she said in a low voice. "That was cruel."

"But it was true. And he knew it."

City Kids

"Why don't you just pin on a label with my name and address?" Miranda said bitterly. "Then I could look like a *complete* infant."

"Will...you...hold...still," Lucy said around the wide taffeta ribbon between her teeth. She finished braiding the thick plait halfway to Miranda's waist and tied on the ribbon with a double knot, creasing the loops between forefinger and thumbnail. "There."

"Hair bows," Miranda groaned. "Bad enough I made my screen debut in a pinafore, now you want to trick me out in hair bows?"

Lucy folded her arms. "You are making me glad I can't go with you this morning," she said. "She's all yours, Robert. You have carfare?"

"Yes, ma'am."

"And the directions?"

Bobby fished a crumpled paper from a pocket. "We pick up the streetcar on Sunset and change at Santa Monica Boulevard. It goes all the way, even though the name changes to Railroad, then Oregon. When we get to Santa Monica, we change to the Ocean Avenue line, and it drops us a few blocks from the gates." He read out: "Walk north up road until sign. I will meet you there and take you to Ince."

"You know this Mr. Ince?" Lucy asked.

"Enough to pick him out of a crowd," Bobby replied. "Face like the map of Ireland, usually wears a sweater instead of a jacket."

"I meant, is he a man of character?"

"Oh, yes. Everyone says so."

"He'd better be," Lucy grumbled. "If you get into trouble ring me, and I'll cancel my lessons and come get you."

"And wheel us home in a pram, no doubt," Miranda said as the front door closed behind them.

Zeb was waiting as promised, and led them up the rutted dirt road that wound into Santa Ynez Canyon, past slopes purple with heather and dotted with the inevitable dusty-looking clumps of sagebrush. "When you come early morning," he told them, "you won't have to walk it. Mule team'll meet you." As they strolled along (Miranda with one ear on the story while she unbraided her hair), Zeb filled them in on the history of the place. It was yet another tangled tale at the heart of which lay, like a snake coiled at the bottom of a water butt, The Motion Picture Patents Company, the infamous consortium formed in 1908 by Thomas Edison and his associates to, as Bobby put it, "keep the picture game all to themselves, the big stinkers."

In 1910, The New York Motion Picture Company leased eighteen thousand acres of what had once been a Spanish rancho called Topanga Malibu Sequit. A

117

year later, when a branch of the company known as Bison Life Motion Picture Company found Edendale no refuge from Al McCoy, the Trust's most hated and feared agent, they took up residence on the barren land. It was a lonely wilderness without drinking water or telephone lines, where coyotes howled in the hills and rattlesnakes lurked in the brush—but the one entrance onto the property could be defended by a few stout fellows with shotguns.

A few miles down the coast, in Venice, the Miller Brothers 101 Ranch Real Wild West Show was giving performances in their arena and shooting Westerns under the hot California sun. The idea of a merger seemed a natural to Thomas Ince, The New York's manager, so he leased additional oceanfront acreage and contracted with the Millers for their entire stock: real live Indians, buffalo, longhorn cattle, pinto ponies, sharpshooters, trick riders, ranch hands, and a handsome black-haired actor named Tom Mix.

"They called 'em 101-Bisons," Zeb said. "We made some big pictures in them days, like *Custer's Last Fight*. Used real Sioux on that one."

"In them days?" Bobby echoed.

"Most of the show moved out last year," he said heavily. "Now it's Kay-Bee and, mama!, are they organized. We shoot eight thousand feet some weeks. No more sleepin' in tents, no more roughin' it. We got dressing rooms and bunkhouses for the hands, all kinds of bushwah." He brightened and added, "We got Bill Hart, though. And we can still do a stampede or a barn-burnin' good as you ever saw."

118

They rounded the last curve and there, flowing across seemingly every inch of flat ground to the base of the mountains, was what appeared to be a small town of decidedly eclectic architecture. A Japanese fishing village clung to the slope of one hill, and Miranda saw the half-timbered cottages of a medieval village huddled at the ankles of a roofless Gothic church. Most of it, however, resembled the towns she had seen from *The Limited*: square buildings with false fronts, saloons with swinging doors, rickety hotels and dance halls, board sidewalks and unpaved streets, horses tied at hitching rails with noses placidly in feedbags. Through a gap in the foothills they could glimpse the stables and corrals, and a line of buckboards, canvas-topped prairie schooners, and stagecoaches. Over it all lay the ripe ammoniac smell of horses, the fresh tang of sawdust and new lumber, and the salty smell of the ocean. The eccentric cacophony of a movie studio— hammering and banging and sawing from sets under construction, shouts and laughter and the din of Victrolas and trios grinding out mood music—rose up and Miranda felt a delightful tingling somewhere under her rib cage. *She was home.*

They threaded their way through the pleasing confusion to the office, which was housed in an unpretentious frame building. A man stood by the entrance, holding a clipboard and watching a band of mustangs being led down the street, their tawny flanks gleaming through a cloud of raised dust. He spotted Zeb and shouted, "Calhoun! What do you think of my new babies?"

"Very fine, sir. We can use 'em, I'm sure." He turned to Bobby and Miranda and said, "Act respectful, now."

"Mr. Ince? These are the kids I ast you about, Robert Gilmer and Miranda Gaines."

The man looked them over briefly. "I'm told you have experience, so I'll assume you can act. Can you ride?"

"Only since I could walk," said Miranda.

"Just watch us," said Bobby.

Ince smiled at them and riffled through the papers on the clipboard until he found what he was looking for. "This should do it," he said to himself; then, addressing Zeb, "Randall's shooting up by the stables this morning. Buckboard of pioneers surrounded by Indians. You know the drill. Get Gilmer and Gaines here—say, that's got a ring to it!—fitted out and have 'em ride behind the wagon.

"Now, you two. See that building over there? Go 'round behind it, third door on the left is wardrobe. Ask for Velda and tell her I said standard settler duds. Then come back here and Zeb'll take you up to the shoot."

"Thank you very much, sir," Bobby said.

"Oh, yes, thank you!" Miranda chimed in, and they turned and walked away. Halfway across the street, high spirits took over and they joined hands and broke into a run, rounding the corner of the building with a leap.

"Thankee kindly, sir," said Zeb. "You won't be sorry."

"Probably not. They seem like good kids."

"What about . . . that other matter?"

"It is a sad truth, my friend, that there are more horses' asses in this world than horses." He sighed. "But he is talented. Donnelly, too, I suppose?"

"The girl did say they were pretty much of a team."

"And I know which one's lead dog." He laughed and clapped Zeb's bony shoulder. "I should send you out as a talent scout, Calhoun."

The morning's shoot was set on a level patch of waste ground, roughly the length of a football field, between the stables and the abrupt ascent of the hills. As Miranda and Bobby and Zeb came over a rise, they could see a small group gathered around the camera. A weathered buckboard was parked nearby, a middle-aged couple seated up front. The man was in shirt-sleeves and suspenders, Levi's, and flat-brimmed hat, his "wife" in a faded calico dress and sunbonnet. There were three young boys in the bed of the wagon, who were passing the time until the scene started by pinching, tickling, and generally annoying each other.

Zeb was leading two bay quarter horses. He handed the reins to Miranda and Bobby, told them to wait, and went to a fellow standing beside the camera. They spoke for a moment, then Zeb motioned them over and introduced them to the director, whose name was Sullivan Randall. Mr. Randall was wearing a pristinely laundered shirt, a Harvard tie, and a dove-gray suit of tropical-weight worsted. A heavy gold signet ring gleamed on a pinkie finger. His hair was brassy gold and waved back from a high brow. Miranda thought he looked exactly like the man in the Arrow collar ads or the kind of square-jawed yachtsman drawn by Charles Dana Gibson.

"Sully here's from back East like yerselves," Zeb said.

"Oh, where?" Miranda said eagerly. "I'm from Leewood Heights, New Jersey. That's near Fort Lee, you know."

The man pushed down his dark glasses with a fingertip and stared at her. His eyes were pale blue and set rather too close together. "I," he said coolly, "am from Boston. Back Bay, actualleh."

"Wouldn't let you into the front part of town, eh?" Bobby quipped. The cameraman, a wizened fellow named Pete Delahanty who would never look like anything other than the ex-jockey he was, snickered rudely, then wisely ducked his head and began to fiddle with the camera.

Sully permitted himself a minuscule smile. "Where are you from, old man?"

Bobby smiled back. "The theatah, old man."

"Then *do* try to contain yourself. We require only the basics here, no grandstanding or showing off."

"Like when I was with the Biograph?" Bobby said amiably.

Sully pushed his glasses back into place and did not answer. "I hope they can ride," he said to Zeb.

"Tom wouldn't have hired 'em unless," he said heartily. "You tell 'em what you want, they'll do it."

"Splendid," Sully said unenthusiastically. "The wagon will go straight down the field. You two ride behind, at a walk. When it reaches that ravine—down there, by the eucalyptus grove—a band of mounted savages will emerge from the trees and surround you. Just follow the wagon and don't improvise.

"If I want the action speeded up for any reason," he continued, "I'll wave my arms in a circle. That means—"

"'Scuse me, sir," said Pete. "You want everyone looking at the camera?"

"Certainly not."

"'Cause if they're watching for your signal—"

"Never mind, then," he said haughtily. "I'll use the megaphone."

"Over here," Zeb said to Miranda and Bobby. "You can mount up by the wagon."

Zeb looked at Miranda curiously as they stood to the rear of the buckboard. Her face was white and there was a faint sheen on her upper lip. He cupped his hands in front of her. "Leg up, honey. Come on."

"What's that thing?" she said, pointing up at the saddle.

"The horn? You ain't never rode Western, have you."

She shook her head.

"Tell me quick and tell me true," he said in a low voice.

"Pony rides at birthday parties."

"Oh brother. What about you, Bob?"

"I was an extra in *The Battle at Elderbrush Gulch*. I fell off and broke my collarbone."

"Listen up and listen good," Zeb said. "Western's easier than them puny English deals. You sit in it like a chair. Use your heels to make the horse go. Tug the reins—gently!—to turn the horse's head in the direction you're aiming. If you have to trot, which ain't likely, squeeze with your knees and try not to bounce up and down too much."

"What about cantering?" Miranda asked.

"To canter on the right lead, pull on the right rein and dig in with your left heel—what'm I sayin'? Don't even think about it!" He smiled reassuringly. "You'll be fine, punkin'. All's you got to do is walk behind a wagon. Relax and enjoy it."

"Relax and enjoy it, relax and enjoy it," Miranda repeated to herself. The saddle was so large and complicated, so wide and heavy and stiff. It seemed to have a life of its own that was somehow connected to the horse while she was perched on it like a cowbird on a holstein. The horse's head seemed a mile away, and the ground was . . . better not to look. For once, she was glad she was not wearing the kind of costume so dear to her dreams of glamour. The gingham shirt, divided skirt, and broken-in boots Velda had given her were comfort itself, and the low-brimmed felt hat with the leather slide, while it did obscure visibility somewhat, kept her hair out of her face.

"Hey, Bobby?"

"What?"

"You scared?"

"My heart stopped beating," he said tersely. "Maybe I'm dead and don't know it."

"Not so loud," she whispered. "Those boys in the wagon are staring at us."

"So's that director," he said glumly. "What a pill!"

"I'll say," she giggled. "The big deal from Bean Town—"

"*Roll camera.*"

Bobby ran a dry tongue over dry lips. "HailMaryfullofgrace—"

"*Action!*"

The buckboard began to inch forward.

Miranda swallowed hard, flapped the reins, and felt for the horse with her heels. Wonder of wonders—it moved into a slow gait, smooth and even as could be. Why, this was a lead-pipe cinch! She glanced over at Bobby. He, too, was moving forward, keeping pace with her and actually grinning a little.

Sully was shouting directions through his megaphone. "Take it slow, take it slow . . . stay in line, stay in line . . . keep it straight. You boys in the wagon—move around a little, don't just sit there like lumps. Look at the scenery . . . show some interest in your surroundings. . . ."

The youngest of the three boys was named Elmer Dickinson, and he was not having a good day. He was seven years old and his mother worked in the wardrobe department. If Granny hadn't had to go to the doctor he'd be home with her now, eating gingerbread men and playing Chinese checkers instead of being an extra because Mama thought it'd be more fun than watching her sew. But it was boring and awful sitting in the back of a wagon while two older boys you didn't even know teased you and called you baby and pinched you when the grown-ups weren't looking. And he'd just noticed there was a splinter in his thumb, a big scary one. Oh, how he wanted to put his hand in his mouth to ease the throbbing, but if those boys caught him sucking his thumb. . . . *I'll make a bandage,* he thought miserably, and pulled a grubby handkerchief out of his pocket. The breeze snatched it out of his hand, and it fluttered out the back of the wagon. Twisting and turning, the white cloth danced directly across the muzzle of Miranda's horse.

Miranda felt an earthquake run beneath her as the horse quivered and bunched its muscles and shied, rearing up briefly on its back legs. It whinnied with fear, tossing its head from side to side, swerved awkwardly around the wagon . . . and bolted!

Miranda grabbed the horn and held on for dear life. The reins were flapping uselessly on the horse's neck, and she could dimly hear, above the wind and panic rushing in her ears like roaring waves of surf, the woman on the buckboard screaming and Bobby's shouts of "Miranda! Miranda, come back, come back!"

Come back? she thought wildly. *Does he think I can steer this thing?*

The trees were whipping past in a blur, like film running through a projector at the wrong speed. She heard the thunder of hooves behind her—the buckboard was in pursuit. Bobby's cries were growing fainter and fainter as the mountains loomed nearer and nearer.

Then, out of the corner of her eye, she saw a tall, leanly muscled Indian on a brown-and-white pony streak out of the eucalyptus stand off to her right. He galloped straight toward her, holding the reins in one hand and standing in his stirrups with superb balance. In a flash, he was by her side, matching her horse's manic loping stride for stride. He was bare chested and wore fringed leather chaps decorated with silver conchas and a beaded headband low on his forehead. Coarse blue-black hair flowed over his shoulders. "Oh, Miss! Miss! I'm gonna grab you!" he shouted into the wind.

"How?" she yelled. She dared a quick glance and, in an instant of clarity, saw that he had very bright blue eyes.

"When I have you," he hollered, "let go!"

"No!"

"Yes!"

"I'm not lettin' go!"

Miranda felt an arm around her waist, pulling her hard to one side, and her left foot lost its tenuous berth in the stirrup. "Get your feet free," her rescuer yelled in her ear.

In for a penny, in for a pound, she thought, and wriggled her right foot out of the stirrup. Immediately, she felt herself being dragged out of the saddle and over the frightening open gap between the horses.

"Now, go limp!" he shouted—and with a thrill of horror she saw him drop his reins and put his other arm around her waist. Before she had the time to question or think or even scream, he threw his left leg over his saddle, pulled her the rest of the way across to the far side, and jumped!

The ground rushed up with sickening speed, and then they were down and rolling over and over and over, coming to rest with the Indian on his back in the dirt. Miranda was lying on top of him. His arms were still tightly around her waist, and she could feel him gasping and heaving beneath her. "Lemme up," she panted. Without a word, he let his arms flop open, and she crawled off his stomach.

Miranda sat up and looked around—the riderless horses were galloping in tandem toward the end of the field, their pace slackening as they lost interest in the contest—then at the Indian. There were pale buff-colored streaks on his reddish brown chest and arms. She looked down and saw that her shirt was streaked with corresponding smears of greasepaint. She took off her hat, threw it down, and pushed her bangs off her forehead.

"*Phew!*" she said. "That was fun."

The Indian opened his eyes and looked up at her. They widened and he let out a low whistle. "You're just a girl!"

"So?" Miranda said testily. "You ain't exactly a real Injun."

He grinned at her, then grabbed his headband and peeled off his wig to reveal a head of wheat brown hair, poker straight and streaked with the sun. "You got me there, Miss."

"Miranda Gaines."

"Jack Bell. Uh-oh, here they come. Mr. Ince, too. We're probably gonna catch hell."

"I don't see why. You saved my life."

"Oh, I don't know about that," he said laconically. "Nag would've run out of steam sooner or later."

"Red! Red!" Bobby came riding down the field at a jangling trot, elbows pumping energetically.

"Look at that poor kid," Jack said pityingly. "He's workin' harder than the horse."

128

Thomas Ince strode up to Jack and reached down to shake his hand. "Bell," he said warmly, "that was as fine a piece of bulldogging as I've seen this year. Good job, man!"

"Thank you, sir, but I honestly didn't know what else to do."

Ince chuckled. "No problem. Listen, Randall," he said as Sully and Zeb came running up. "I want all this in. Make Gilmer the brother. He and Gaines get captured by Bell here and dragged off with the rest of the wagon party."

Bobby slid to the ground and gratefully handed the reins to Zeb. "That means we finish the day?" he said to Ince.

"Finish the week, kid. Then you and Gaines come 'round to the office and we'll see what we can do."

"That's not what was in the scenario," Sully whined.

"There's no picture so good it can't be changed," Ince replied cheerfully. "As all my *assistant directors* well know."

Bobby and Miranda exchanged a look of pure vindication: Assistant director? Hah!

"Never look a runaway gift horse in the mouth, boys," said Thomas Ince. He rocked back on his heels, stuck his thumbs in his belt loops, and gazed happily at the chaos this one unremarkable two-reel oater had caused. The buckboard leaned drunkenly over the narrow gully edging the field, the horses lathered and drooping. One of the little boys in the back of the wagon was bawling and sucking his thumb. The Indians had come out of their ambush and milled about

129

the kids on the ground, who were sweaty, filthy, streaked with dirt and greasepaint, and laughing their heads off. That high-handed nabob the money boys in New York had forced on him stood cracking his knuckles, unaware of a three-cornered tear in the seat of his Brooks Brothers trousers through which his lemon silk shorts protruded. Ah, but life was good!

By the end of the day the friendship of Miranda and Bobby and Jack was set in cement. Nothing, they swore solemnly, would part The Three Musketeers of Inceville. It was a bond based in part on the fact that they were ridiculously young, even for a business where a director could be termed an old hand at twenty-five, and in part on the lightning-quick recognition of their mutual masquerade. To varying degrees they were all, as Bobby said bluntly, "faking it."

Miranda had told everyone she was fifteen, Bobby had blithely stated they could ride like the wind, and Jack's employment with Kay-Bee had been predicated on his rodeo experience—of which, in fact, he had none.

"I've been roping and cutting since I was in short pants," he said by way of explanation. "Just not in front of a camera."

Their pact was sealed with the standard spit-and-a-handshake behind the Main Street saloon. Jack would teach Miranda and Bobby enough basic riding skills to keep them on horseback and the payroll, and Bobby offered to help Jack with his acting. "I'm not going to say teach," Bobby said earnestly, "because it's my personal contention no one can teach anyone how to act. But I can show you a trick or two. Including"—

and he grinned slyly—"how to hog the camera should you ever get the chance."

"I watched you today, and at first I thought you weren't doing anything. It seemed so low-key," said Jack. "Some of the actors 'round here..." He shook his head.

"Those hambones?" Bobby laughed. "Old-time stage tricks don't make the grade in the picture game. It's like this, Jack. By the time your handsome pan hits the silversheet, you're ten feet tall and your head's the size of a washtub. A nice big smile will make you look like the village idiot."

"Keep it simple?"

"As C.J. would say, got it in one."

They wrapped at four when Pete judged the light was getting yellow. The late afternoon sun cast too many shadows and softened images with hazy coronas: Anything filmed then would be impossible to match to footage shot in the stark glare of noon. It was the hour the more artistically inclined—like Jerry Donnelly and his former mentor, Billy Bitzer—called "Golden Time" and waited for, but at Inceville it heralded quitting time.

"Anyone waitin' on you?" Jack queried, as they dismounted and prepared to lead their horses to the corral.

Miranda looked at Bobby. "She probably won't expect us till six or so, don't you think?"

"She'd have no way of knowing. Whether or not we were working, I mean," Bobby reasoned.

"My aunt," Miranda explained to Jack. "Bobby and I live with her."

"Wait here. I'll go clear it," Jack said mysteriously. "Hold my reins, Bob." He walked off toward the stables.

As soon as he was out of sight, Miranda bent over and began to massage her calf muscles. "I...am... so...*sore*," she moaned.

"I feel," Bobby said vehemently, "like I been dropped off a building. Feet first."

"We really are a couple of city kids."

"I never claimed to be anything else. Calamity Miranda! 'Oh, I've been riding since I could walk,'" he mimicked. "I'll tell you one thing: We grin and bear it. I spent enough time before you got here sitting outside studios—getting bombed with goo from those dratted pepper trees, I might add—to know there's a long line behind us just itching for us to fail."

"The more we work, the more— Here he comes."

"Hot baths," Jack said as he walked up to them. "Soak in a hot bath tonight, as hot as you can stand, and rub in all the Sloane's liniment your skin will hold. That'll help." He took the reins from Bobby and mounted in one graceful, practiced motion. "So will this."

"You mean that old saw about getting back on the horse?" Miranda said with despair.

"Up-up," Jack said with a grin. "You, too, Gilmer."

"I'm going back to the theater," Bobby panted, holding the horn and reins with one hand while he attempted to lift his foot to the stirrup with the other. He got a toehold, then heaved himself across the saddle with a pained grunt. He threw his leg over, got his foot safely into the stirrup on the far side, and laid his head down on the horse's neck. "Smelly dressing rooms," he moaned. "Cold and cold running water, cracked mirrors. It'll be heaven."

"Next time try the fence," Jack said. He reached over to Miranda's horse, took the reins, and led it to the split-rail surrounding the corral. "No shame in that. Come on, Randa."

"Oh, that's much easier," said Miranda. "Thanks, Jack. Where are we going?"

"Up the canyon," he replied. "Take it slow, a nice easy walk. The horses know more than you think they do."

"They couldn't know any less than we do," Miranda said.

"You're learning," he called over his shoulder. "You're learning."

They picked their way up into the sagebrush, the sounds of Inceville fading behind them until they were high on a ridge, riding along the very spine of Santa Ynez Canyon. The air was thick with the pungent scent of the pines and the aromas of bruised sage and the sunbaked dust that rose from their tracks. Miranda's spirit seemed to lift to the hard, clear sky above, her aching muscles easing into the rocking-chair tempo of the horse. Jack rode to a secluded spot overlooking the ocean, dismounted, and tied up to a gnarled piñon. He pulled a bunch of dried grass and began to wipe down his horse, who whickered softly and nuzzled his shirtfront.

"This is pretty," exclaimed Miranda as she rode up. "I used to think everything looked so bare compared to home, but I'm getting used to it. It's as if you can see the bones of the earth."

133

"When spring comes, these hills will be covered with flowers," he said as he helped her dismount. "Wild roses, lupines, poppies. Indian paintbrush, mariposa lilies, strange plants that grow right out of the rocks. Doesn't last long, but it's worth the wait."

"How do you know all this?" she asked curiously.

He gazed around him and smiled, the corners of his eyes crinkling. "I love the land," he said simply.

"Wouldn't it be wonderful to live up here? To have that view every day."

"Put out your hands." He took a fistful of dirt and let it trickle into her open palms. "Spread your fingers—see? Goes right through. No one's ever going to build in these canyons. The earth is too loose. The rains would carry anything you put up here straight into the ocean."

Miranda watched the powdery soil sift through her fingers and feather away. "I'm glad," she said shyly. "I'd hate to see it spoiled."

"Me, too. For one thing, it's the best place I know to indulge in a fine old western tradition—watching the sunset."

"We do that back East, you know."

"I'm sure you do. But not with a campfire, I'll bet."

Bobby appeared over the lip of the ridge. "Campfire?" he said hopefully. "Food?"

"Naw," said Jack. "You watch the flames and talk about life."

"Oh, deliver me."

There was plenty of dry wood and brush for kindling, and within minutes they were sitting around a small fire that cracked and popped with pine sap. "Don't ever use eucalyptus," Jack instructed. "Stuff's full of oil, goes up like Roman candles. It ain't from around here, you know. Some fool imported it from Australia."

"Why?" asked Miranda.

"Grows fast." He leaned his back against a rock and stretched out his long legs. "Ladies first. How'd you get into pictures, Randa?"

She eyed Bobby and they snickered. "I guess you could say I just fell into it." And she launched into the story of The American Moving Picture Company hiding from the Trust in the sleepy little town of Leewood Heights, bound and determined to make a five-reel feature with their last dime—

"She was snoopin'," Bobby cut in, "and fell right smack into the shot. Nearly broke my neck. The rest, as they say, is history."

"C.J. put me in the picture," Miranda went on, "and I had to sneak around all summer so Auntie wouldn't find out, but she did anyway, and then we all had to convince her to come out West so I could be in pictures, and that's that, I guess."

"Till she drags you back come Christmas," Bobby said sourly.

"*What?*" she whispered.

"Me and my big mouth." Bobby ran a hand through his hair. "The Boss let slip. He and Lucy struck a bargain: one year. You got until Christmas Day."

Miranda clenched her fists. "And then?"

"I don't know," he said, and shrugged. "Then she decides."

"A lot can happen in a year," said Jack.

"Hey, we got her out here," said Bobby. "That's a

135

miracle in itself. Piece of cake to make her stay. Besides," he added with a grimace, "if you two leave, I'll have to go back to living with C.J."

A slow smile lit Miranda's face. "That's right. She'd be throwin' a poor orphan boy into the street—"

"Not again!" Bobby said with a laugh. "We've used that one till it's got whiskers."

"We'll think of something. At least now I know where I stand."

"Looking at the set of your jaw," Jack remarked, "is enough to make me feel sorry for the woman. Okay, Gilmer, your turn."

"Grew up in the theater. My mother died when I was thirteen."

"What about your dad?" said Jack.

"Never knew him," Bobby said curtly. "Probably didn't miss much." That, he had long since decided, was undoubtedly the case. His mother's stories had changed with her mood, the amount of alcohol consumed, and the town they were playing. A two-week engagement in New Orleans, for instance, had elicited an improbable tale of a dark-haired gentleman with the manners of a prince and five hundred acres in cotton along the Mississippi. The men in the stories were always tall and dark. Given his own dark hair and slim build, that much, Bobby surmised, was true. After a while he'd stopped asking.

"I used to work at the Biograph, in New York. Hooked up with C.J. when he started The American."

"That's it?" Jack said.

"That's it."

"Your turn, Jack," Miranda said quickly.

John Scott Bell was eighteen, born and raised on a small ranch an hour's hard ride east of Billings, Montana. His father had been killed two years previous in a hunting accident—a shotgun improperly loaded had discharged into his chest, he told them. He did not tell them of leaping onto his horse and riding hell-for-leather for the doctor while, in a wooded copse on the slope of the blue foothills, his father's life ebbed slowly into the dust. Nor did he tell them of the year he and his mother and three sisters had struggled to keep the old place going, nor of their anguished decision to sell up. "Ma's a teacher," he said simply. "She and the girls live in Billings now."

"A schoolmarm?" said Miranda.

"All the West ain't a dime novel. She teaches English literature and composition in the district high school. It's a three-story brick building with four athletic fields, a science laboratory good as the university's, and an orchestra that plays for assembly every morning."

"You're breakin' her heart," Bobby said.

"Another illusion shattered." Miranda sighed. "Tell me about your sisters."

"Ruby's sixteen, Tess is fourteen, and Susie's nine. Good girls," he said fondly. "Of course, they talk too much, like someone else I know."

"How'd you end up here?" Bobby asked.

"Money," Jack replied. "And Tom Mix."

"Ooh," Miranda breathed. "You know Tom Mix?"

"No more than anyone else with the price of admission. I was sittin' in the Bijou watching one of his pictures, and Ruby leans over and whispers, 'You ride

as good as he does, Jackie.' And I thought, Darned if I
don't."

"Money?" Miranda prompted.

Jack picked up a stick and poked the fire. "I'm saving up to buy back our ranch."

"So that's why—," Bobby said, and stopped.

"Why what?"

"Zeb told us you take on every fool stunt they
offer."

"I'm not looking to break my neck. You get twenty
extra for overturning a wagon at full speed and fifteen
for dragging behind a horse."

"Buy a lotta dogies with that kinda scratch," Miranda drawled, and pretended to spit into the fire.

Bobby rolled his eyes, but Jack laughed. "You're a
pistol, Randa. Want to race?"

"You're practically six feet tall! I hardly call that
fair."

"Six two. Not on foot, you goofus. Down there—"
and he pointed to the shore, just beyond the coast
road winding along the base of the hills.

"You mean the beach?" Miranda asked excitedly.
"Race along the beach?"

"I don't know," Bobby said doubtfully. "I'm not
sure I can even get back up on Old Paint there without screaming."

"I ain't gonna kill ya," Jack said in an exaggerated
western drawl. "What the heck would I do for laughs?"

The sun was dropping rapidly now, turning the
sky to purple and staining the undersides of the clouds
with brilliant orange light. A broad path of gold

streamed across the water, and the headlands burned crimson in the reflected glow.

They raked the fire to cold ash and buried it, then untethered the horses and made their way down the slope and across the road. Shore birds were twittering in the tall grass, and the air had turned chill with the twilight. They followed Jack onto the beach in single file, listening to the waves lapping lazily against the shore, the jingle of bit and bridle, the saddles rubbing and squeaking with the rhythm of the horses. The lights of Santa Monica were a string of glittering jewels on the horizon behind them, and they could hear, coming in short snatches on the breeze, the faint carnival strains of hurdy-gurdy music from the pier.

They reached an outcropping of rock and lined up three abreast. The sand lay before them, a wide dramatic crescent marked only with their hoofprints. The moment stretched, hushed, a thread of tension pulled taut. . . .

Jack stood in his stirrups, reins gathered in one hand, his hat held high in the other. "All for one and one for all!" His arm slashed downward. "Go!"

They dug their heels in and the startled horses burst forward, rending the soft dusk with the thunder of hoofbeats as they pounded down the beach. Miranda and Bobby were no match for Jack after one short day in the saddle, but, miraculously, they managed to hang on, laughing and whooping breathlessly. Miranda's hair streamed behind her, copper turned to flame by the setting sun, a regimental banner flying over the cavalry's last charge.

Beer, and the Possibility
of Champagne

S ummer was a path with no turnings, as straight
and true as the rail lines across the desert. The
parched days slid one into the next, June gone in
heat and dust, July a shimmering blur, and it was August. They were settled now into the frantic routine
that was Inceville, the long action-crammed days as
natural as school had been to Miranda, and eight
shows a week to Bobby.

Up with the dawn, each as clear as the one before
or the one to come. Throw some breakfast down your
throat, stuff the rest in your pocket for the trolley ride
to Santa Monica, the excitement mounting as you
neared the sea and caught the first whiff of its wild
briny smell and spotted the seagulls wheeling against
the sky. Walk up the coast road to the gates to catch
the wagon up the winding, rutted road to the studio,
get the day's assignments off the board, dive into
makeup and wardrobe, then on to the set for a dizzying
succession of bit parts and extra work.

No time to discuss character development or the
meaning of each scene. This was filmmaking with all

the spontaneity of Henry Ford's assembly line—pictures were shot, edited, and in the can in less than two weeks. It was a disciplined whirlwind, and although Miranda did not realize it at the time, it was training that compressed the lessons of a lifetime into a few short months.

One day you were a Russian princess in a vile-smelling velvet gown with tarnished embroidery and a dragging hem, throwing yourself around a platform stage while the studio musicians sawed away at "The Volga Boatmen" and the backdrop ruffled in the breeze.

"If it's supposed to be an interior, how is it going to look if the walls are moving?" Miranda had asked Bobby, who was braving the ninety-degree heat in the fur hat, wool tunic, and thigh boots of a Cossack.

"Aw, they'll be so busy watching your awful emoting they won't notice if the walls are bleeding" was his reply—quickly disarmed with a grin, for her arm was back, fist clenched to strike.

Russian princesses or, to be exact, the younger sister of the lead Russian princess. Lolloping schoolgirls with pigtails wired straight out and painted freckles—how Miranda hated that! French peasant girls with grubby head scarves, grease-spotted aprons, and wooden sabots that raised blisters after two takes. Limpid young damsels in soiled satins and itchy cotton-wool wigs imprisoned aboard *The Fremont*, the decrepit brigantine sagging at anchor offshore. And cowgirls. Simply hundreds of cowgirls.

Cowgirls on horseback, cowgirls in prairie schooners, cowgirls in one-room schoolhouses, cowgirls crouched behind rocks shooting black powder wads from perilously rusty Remington rifles, cowgirls captured by blue-eyed greasepainted Apaches from Ohio, cowgirls tied up and left screaming around smudge-pot campfires, cowgirls homesteading in crude cabin sets, cowgirls running barefoot in artfully tattered clothing down canvas-and-board Main Streets to warn the sheriff. Cowgirls, cowgirls, cowgirls!

Ah, the Girls of Inceville's Golden West, always in the same checked shirt and bandanna neckerchief, the same divided skirt and gun belt, the same dusty laced-up boots, the same wide-brimmed felt hat slung low. And Miranda, who had once lusted after the cowgirl costume she had seen on an actress in a Fort Lee studio as Schliemann lusted after Troy, was tiring of it.

"Why don't they just go ahead and put my name on these rotten duds?" she complained one afternoon to Zeb, who was setting the stunts on her third two-reeler in as many days. "It's not like the part changes from one picture to the next. And why have they got me playing grown-ups, anyway?" Not that she wasn't secretly pleased.

"You're small, punkin'," Zeb said, as he gave her a leg up onto a spavined old gelding (who was dreaming in vain of a quiet roll in the corral). "Always got to have the lady smaller'n the gent, and some of them actors is kinder puny. Slap enough paint on, any gal could pass for a fancy woman. Even a squirt like you."

Miranda did wonder why they were still "cranking them out." *The Clansman* was supposed to have changed all that—or so C.J. had been saying, repeatedly and with mounting despair, in the months since the premiere. Retitled *The Birth of a Nation*, Griffith's epic was in nationwide release, and each week *Variety* reported profits so staggering that keeping an accurate accounting was like trying to race a flash flood down a gully. "It is like writing history with lightning," President Wilson had said of the picture, the first ever to be shown at the White House. The National Association for the Advancement of Colored People thought differently, however, and picketed vigorously. ("More power to you," Lucy said grimly upon reading the story in the morning paper, and she mailed them a contribution that same day.) *The Birth* was banned in a number of cities, including Chicago. Moving pictures, it seemed, had power: proved by the blood flowing in the streets of Boston and Atlanta, proved by the fortunes amassed by those who had purchased distributorships, and proved in the Midwest and the South by unsettling signs that the Ku Klux Klan, once outlawed and reviled, had found new resolve in the darkened hush of a theater. There was no going back.

But, after all that sweep and grandeur and emotion, here they were, grinding away at the kind of program fillers over which Griffith had left the Biograph, and C.J. had left Griffith. She finally approached Bobby one day, and his reasoning was characteristically sane.

"I see it this way," he said thoughtfully, gazing over her head into the distance. "*The Birth* was champagne. You don't drink champagne every day, right? And you don't want to have to go through all that every time you go to a picture show. Feeling like your guts are being kicked in, I mean. People go to pictures to relax, and they drink beer every day. My guess is we're beer."

The trip home at sundown was a release, time to unwind as they hashed over the small and large moments of the day's shoot. Jack made the journey with Miranda and Bobby more nights than not. His boardinghouse was dull as ditchwater, he said, and the food didn't have a patch on Miss Lucy's table. By midsummer Lucy was setting four places for supper without a second thought. They would walk home from the streetcar in the soft dusk, the harsh sunbaked colors of the day dimming to purple and blue and gray as an unseen stagehand played over the light board, the air scented with the neighborhood gardens and the everpresent underlying tang of eucalyptus and wild sage in the hills. Children tired from a day at adult play, they would walk slowly, sometimes swinging lazy circles around the lampposts, often arm in arm. The lights would be on in the little bungalow at the end of the block, and the boys would always have a teasing remark ready for Lucy by the time the screen door banged shut behind them.

It was all very satisfying, as satisfying to Miranda as the passbook she took down to the bank every Saturday morning with her pay envelope. Although her salary was paid directly to Lucy, she had insisted Miranda open a savings account and allowed her to keep out just two dollars each week for sundries, which to Miranda meant Edgar Rice Burroughs and Zane Grey. "I read all the time—I'm always carrying around a book" was her defense whenever Lucy nagged her about the home-study course. "Tarzan does not count as natural science" was Lucy's bemused response. "Or geography, for that matter."

144

By September Miranda had quite a snug balance. She had plans for it, too, and although she knew better than to broach the subject with Lucy, the Christmas Eve bargain weighed heavily. If Auntie made the awful decision to decamp back to the financial security and boredom of Leewood Heights...money meant escape, money and the railway timetables she hid in her bottom bureau drawer under a stack of chemises. Lucy did seem settled enough in their little house, and her reputation and roster of pupils were growing steadily, but she was still given to the kind of offhand remarks that froze Miranda's blood in her veins: "Oh, I can't wait to get back to my own stove so I can cook a proper meal..." "The closets in this house are so skinchy it's like living on a boat..." "I miss the East..." "I miss my friends..." "I miss our day trips to New York, darling, don't you?" *Money,* reasoned Miranda with the maturity that burst forth in her now and again like dandelions spangling a lawn, *is freedom.*

One night toward the middle of October, Miranda—who should have long since been asleep but had smuggled a flashlight into bed to finish off *Rupert of Hentzau*—heard footsteps in the yard. She crawled out from beneath the covers and held her breath as the footsteps went down along the side of the house, around to the back, and stopped at Bobby's room. A handful of dirt was flung at his window. When the noise died away, she heard the protesting screech of the sash being raised.

"All clear?" a voice whispered.

She heard a grunt of acknowledgment, followed by

the soft thud of someone dropping from the window to the grass below.

Quickly, Miranda slipped across her bedroom and dashed down the hall to the front door. She crept down the steps and to the end of the porch and knelt behind the hydrangea bush. When the moment came, she tensed her muscles and sprang into a fierce approximation of the jeté she had once labored over in ballet class. *Madame Gouboutska should see this!* she thought as she landed with a triumphant shriek in front of Bobby and Jack.

"Holy cow!" Bobby yelped as he stumbled backward.

"*Sssssshhh!*" Jack hissed at him.

"I thought she was a ghost," Bobby said in a strangled whisper.

Miranda stood and brushed the dirt off her nightgown. "And just where do you two think you're going?" she said as she folded her arms at her waist, for a moment looking very much like her aunt.

"Nowhere much, Randa, honey," Jack said.

"Don't you 'Randa honey' *me*," she said tartly.

"We weren't goin' nowhere," Bobby said defensively.

"Not without me you weren't."

"Cut me some slack, Red," he pleaded. "You know darn well Lucy'd kill me if she found out we'd let you run all over Griff— Aw, nuts."

"One cat neatly out of the bag," Jack said mildly.

"You were going over to the Fine Arts lot," said Miranda.

No reply.

"In the middle of the night."

"Now, Randa—," Jack began.

"You let me come with you," she said, "or I will start screaming this very minute. Ooh, I can just see it. Lights going on, dogs barking, Auntie running out of the house with her hair in curlers. You won't get to the end of the block."

"Okay, okay," Bobby said testily. "Go put on some clothes. We ain't takin' you nowhere half nekkid."

"If you're not here when I get back," Miranda said over her shoulder as she marched across the lawn, "I'm callin' the police."

"Bossy little thing, ain't she?" Jack commented.

"Not really," Bobby replied. "She just can't stand bein' left out of the action."

They walked down to the corner of Hollywood and Sunset, guided by the streetlamps but careful to avoid the pools of light lest they be seen. Miranda's heart was beating rapidly, and she clenched her fists with suppressed excitement. Who cared if they found nothing but an empty studio? To be out and about in the middle of the night with two boys—two older boys!— was Adventure with a capital A.

"So why tonight?" she whispered when they reached the corner.

"Haven't you noticed that?" Jack said. He pointed across Hollywood Boulevard to a vast bulk looming over the frame buildings of the Fine Arts lot. "I've been watchin' for weeks now. Somethin' big's going on, and I aim to find out what."

"I just assumed they were putting up another

building," said Miranda. "It seems like they're always building *something*."

"Out of scaffolding and canvas? We reckon it's a set."

"Some sort of castle," Bobby added. "It looked like stone towers from the streetcar. We scoped the lay of the land last week, and there's a place in the fence we can get through."

When they had successfully negotiated the gap in the chain-link fence, they found the sort of bustle that characterized Inceville at high noon. The lights were on in many of the ramshackle buildings that were crammed onto the wedge-shaped plot of land. Men scurried about toting camera equipment and big canvas light reflectors and ropes, calling out to each other in the self-important lingo of overworked, underpaid professionals. The night wind eddied about the alleys and passageways, blowing spumes of grit into the air. Miranda was tailing Bobby and Jack around the corner of a shed when two men ran by, churning up plumes of dust with their heels. She flattened herself against the wall as they tore by, and she heard one of the men yell, "We're gonna have to deadman the whole blasted thing if this wind don't ease up!"

"Deadman?" said Miranda.

"Deadmen are lines," Bobby explained. "Ropes to tie down the set. You tie the ropes to railroad ties, then bury the ties. Like they were dead, see?"

They found an observation post around the side of an unlit building and watched as throngs of extras streamed past. There were no women in the crowd, and most of the men Miranda saw were dressed in crude armor vests over rough knee-length tunics, and boots or laced-up sandals. Many wore shoulder-length wigs of tightly bunched curls and flowing crimped-wool beards, and carried spears and shields or wicked-looking spiked clubs.

"I don't get it," Jack said. "I thought this picture was called *The Mother and the Law*. A modern photoplay, that's what the papers are saying. With Mae Marsh and Robert Harron."

"That's what it says on the banner out front," Miranda said. "*The Mother and the Law*."

"Aw, use your noggins," Bobby said with an air of superiority. "You think a studio this big shoots one picture at a time? Just going past here the last couple of months I've seen mill workers and thugs, and people dressed up as French aristocrats, and a *ton* of Bible types. Surely you don't think they'd all be in the same picture."

"Guess not," Jack agreed. "Say, this is getting boring just standing here." He put his head out, then quickly withdrew it. "*Whew!*" He whistled. "You aren't going to believe this. It's *enormous*. Come on!"

They crept out of their dark corner and edged along the buildings, following the stream of extras toward the northwest corner of the property. Here was more purposeful activity than Miranda had ever seen in a studio; assistants dashed here and there, shouting and waving colored signal flags, herding the costumed extras like Border collies nipping the ankles of errant sheep. Banks of working lights aimed skyward cast monstrous and elongated shadows, lending the scene the surreal quality of a nightmare.

A massive set had been constructed, backed against the very edge of the lot (off to one side, the immense mass of an even larger set could be glimpsed beyond the lighted work area). Flanked by mighty square towers painted to simulate slave-cut stone, the stone walls rose into the air, silhouetted against the star-filled sky. In the center of the walls were impressive carved doors, several stories high, which thundered and shuddered agonizingly as stagehands hauled on the mechanism to close them. As Miranda and Bobby and Jack edged into the last row of the crowd, they heard a man in a flowing beard say to a companion, "If Babylon didn't look like this, buddy, you can paint me green and call me a pickle."

"Babylon?" Bobby said with a frown. "*The Mother and the Law* is about Babylon?"

And that is what it was, a miracle wrought by hundreds of carpenters and plasterers and painters. Lofting to a height of ninety feet—as tall as an eight-story building—and with parapets wide enough on which to drive two horse-drawn chariots abreast stood the massive gates of the walled city of Babylon. But here, unlike that ancient marvel of engineering and labor, the walls were rendered in pipe and board and painted canvas, and plaster mixed with bales of horsehair to keep it from cracking in the desert climate.

As it dawned on them that no one was going to remark on—or even notice—their presence, Miranda and the two boys worked their way to the front of the crowd. There they discovered a pile of boxes and scrap lumber and crouched behind it in a tangle of shadow.

"This is the life," Jack whispered. "Front row at the picture show."

The extras had been herded into a flat, open area in front of the set. As an assistant shouted instructions through a megaphone, half of the men began to climb to the top of the walls using ladders and ramps at the far ends of the set. Two attack towers, which were heavy square wooden structures as high as the main walls and connected at the top with hinged walkways, were being moved into position before the doors.

"Look!" Miranda cried.

Bobby clapped a hand over her mouth. "Quiet!" he hissed. "I see 'em."

Miranda pushed his hand away and leaned out of their hiding place. "Elephants?"

"Kind of hard to miss, ain't they?" Jack said with a grin.

As wranglers shouted hoarsely and tapped their flanks with quirts, the two elephants lowered their mammoth heads and gently butted the attack towers forward. When the towers were in place, the elephants stood patiently, slowly shifting their thick feet in the dust.

"Remember Nebuchadnezzar from Sunday school, Randa?" said Jack. "Well, he built walls around Babylon to protect the city from invaders. Worked for a while. Then, in—oh, I can't remember, some time around 540 B.C., I think—when Belshazzar was king of the Persians, Cyrus, who was the king of the Medes—"

"Hang on," Miranda interrupted. "You talking about the Medes and the Persians?"

"Never could keep them straight," Bobby said.

"Me, neither," said Miranda.

"Be that as it may," Jack said. "I'd say we were in for the Fall of Babylon."

"Why shoot it at night?" Miranda asked.

"Probably one of those battles that went on for days," Bobby said. "Or maybe this is just more dramatic."

"There must be a thousand men out there," Jack said.

"More, I'd say," Bobby said, again adopting the superior tone of experience. "A big set like that just devours extras."

"Where's Mr. Griffith?" Miranda said. "I don't see him anywhere."

"Oh, he'll show," Bobby answered. "This is too big to leave to any old assistant direc—" He broke off and emitted a low whistle. "Hot diggety! Fireworks is here." He nudged her and pointed to a man threading his way through the crowd. The man was short and slight and wore a dark beard trimmed to a point. "That's Fireworks Wilson. He does all Griffith's pyrotechnics. Explosions, like that."

"Dangerous job," Jack commented. "Poor guy's missin' an arm."

"Yeah, how 'bout that?" Bobby said. "Everyone says he knows what he's doing, but I'll lay you even money it weren't bit off by no alligator."

The extras on the ground were moved into position at the foot of the doors, and as though Moses had waved his arms above the Red Sea, a wide swath was cleared in front of the twenty-foot-high wooden camera platform that was set some fifteen yards back. The aimless chatter from hundreds of throats began to abate into whispers. A voice drifted out over the scene, coming from the group atop the camera platform—a deep baritone with the unmistakable whiplash of authority cloaked by a rich, lazy-sounding southern drawl.

"Oh, Monte," said the voice. "All in place?"

A sleek-looking fellow in shirtsleeves loped across the open space toward the platform, and Miranda saw, with a thrill that widened her eyes, that he had *two* revolvers stuck in his belt.

"Yes, sir," Monte answered.

"Rats," Miranda muttered savagely. "I can't see him. I can't see Griffith."

"Pipe down, you," said Bobby.

"Ready, Billy?" said the voice.

"Bitzer." Bobby sighed happily. "Good old Billy."

"Yes, sir," a guttural voice replied. "Ready."

Monte Blue stepped into the clearing, raised his arm, and fired a single shot.

All over the great set, along the walls and atop the parapets and down the sides of the towers at regular intervals, fuses began to glow.

Monte looked back up at the platform and, at a signal from D. W. Griffith, fired two shots in rapid succession.

Light leaped to life all over the set, creeping over the great facade like tongues of fire, slow at first then catching and growing into a great flaring burst of brilliant incandescence that seemed to set the very sky aglow.

"I don't believe it," Bobby breathed. "He's lightin' the thing with *flares*."

Three shots from Monte Blue's revolvers...and the battle erupted in a blast of screaming noisy clangor, a furious din of metal on metal and men shouting and yelling at the top of their lungs as they stormed the walls, and thunderous groans as the elephants pushed the attack towers nearer and nearer. Men were crawling over the top of the walls, shrieking like banshees and hitting each other with clubs and swords and their fists. Over the enormous doors, which were ringing and shaking under the assault of a thousand blows, men were tipping a large cauldron of liquid—boiling oil!—onto the hapless attackers below.

Miranda and the two boys were on their feet now, jumping up and down, screaming and laughing hysterically with the sheer madness of it all. "Get 'em, get 'em!" Jack was yelling, and Bobby was whooping madly, imitating the rebel yells of *The Birth*.

"Like the wolf on the fold," Miranda babbled excitedly. "The Assyrian came down like the wolf on the fold!"

Just when the boiling furious clamor had reached a manic, reckless, overwhelming crescendo...the flares went out. A great yell went up and the extras froze in place, suspended, blinded, waiting for their eyes to adjust—first to the darkness, then to the banks of working lights below. It was over. Light to dark, the entire shot had lasted only three minutes.

Miranda stared wordlessly at Bobby, then Jack. Jack's jaw hung slack. Bobby was panting as though he'd been running, and grinning from ear to ear.

The voice came from the platform: "Thank you. All for tonight."

"That's all?" Miranda said, her shoulders sagging with disappointment. "Oh, rats."

"Naw, that ain't all," Bobby said firmly. "We're coming back. Next time we get a few days off, we're comin' back. We'll get jobs as extras. I'd say by the look of things there'll be plenty to go around."

Miranda stared at him. "We're doin' parts now. Why go back to extra work?"

"Because, you little ham, this is history, and I aim to be a part of it. If we can get a few days off—"

"We can't," Miranda said. "I saw the schedule for next week. It's cowboys 'n' Indians from dawn to dusk." She sighed. "It would be nice to just walk around in costume for a few days and not gallop all over the place. I don't fall off much anymore, but I still get awful sore."

"Lucy," Bobby said with a slow grin. "We'll blame it on Lucy. We'll say she's nervous about us truckin' all the way out to the beach and wants us to work closer to home for a bit. C.J. can cover for us; he'll understand. You in, Jack?"

"And how."

"Red?"

"What do you think!"

Babylon, My Babylon

Higher and higher, rising to the thin aquamarine sky, the glory of Belshazzar rose above the humble bungalows and scrubland of Hollywood. The set Miranda had discerned in the madness of midnight as a hulking mass beyond the gate was now revealed, shimmering and baking in the flat California sun, on the morning she and Bobby and Jack reported for their first day as extras in what was to become *Intolerance*, surely the biggest—and surely the greatest!—moving picture ever made.

Miranda gasped as her eyes were drawn up . . . and up . . . and up.

"Holy Mother," Bobby said in a muted voice.

"I wish Jer' could see this," Miranda said wistfully. "He's never around much anymore."

"Working two jobs now," Bobby said absently, his eyes following hers skyward. "He's saving up for another camera in case Baby ever breaks. Say, ain't that something?"

"You were right, Bob," Jack said. "This *is* history."

To say the main Babylon set was large was an under-

156

statement. It was *huge*. Gleaming white structures with ziggurat-shaped entrances flanked a gentle rise of stairs leading up to a vast open boulevard that was broad enough to accommodate any triumphal procession or invading army. Atop the buildings, staircases lined with statues of menacing animal-headed men and lions and strange beasts of antiquity led to elegant balconies, where extras milled about and waved to the peons below. Huge round pillars supported a second tier of balconies festooned with hieroglyphs and more beasts and filled with more richly costumed extras. Rising from the top balconies was the final wondrous touch—great plump rococo plaster elephants, as white as paper, their curled trunks lifting in proud repeat, stretching away into the background where, through immense formal archways hung with banners, the inescapable surround of parched hills lay against the horizon.

This was no slapdash affair of board and canvas thrown up and daubed with the casual assumption that the camera's ruthless eye would somehow overlook any imperfection. Everywhere Miranda looked she saw skillful painting, the glittering magnificence of gilt, and the lush earthy colors of terra-cotta and ocher, and Nile green and crimson.

She nudged Bobby, who was still standing next to her with his mouth open, reverence putting a flush to his cheeks and a shine to his cat-green eyes. "Too bad film is black and white," she said.

"You want to hand-tint every frame of *that?*" He waved a gesture encompassing the amazing scene from the dust at their feet to the banners fluttering crisply atop the farthest tower, nearly a quarter of a mile away. He put a hand up to shade his eyes. "Color'd be too confusing," he said, squinting professionally. "You need the clarity of black and white."

"Yessir, Mr. Bitzer, sir," Miranda said witheringly. "It was only a suggestion."

"What's your assignment, Bob?" Jack said tactfully, consulting the scrap of paper in his hand. "Me, I'm your basic citizen of good old Babylon. I'm supposed to stand at the base of those steps over there and carry on like I'm having the time of my life."

"Me, too," said Bobby. "Where are you supposed to be, Red?"

"With the dancers from the Denishawn School of Dance," Miranda said smugly.

"Hoo-eee." Bobby whistled. "How'd you manage that?"

"The man just looked at me and asked if I'd had any dance training, so of course I said yes."

"Not like you had riding lessons, I hope," Jack said.

"No," she said, grinning at him. "All those rotten ballet lessons are finally going to pay off."

"Ted Shawn and Ruth St. Denis don't go in much for ballet," Bobby said. "I saw them once in Chicago. They sort of fling themselves about. They don't even point their toes."

"The man said they needed someone my size to fill out one of the lines," Miranda told him. "He said all I had to do was watch what the others were doing and copy them."

"You know what I heard?" Bobby asked. "We aren't gonna rehearse."

"What?" Miranda and Jack said in unison.

"Nope. Everyone'll be told where to go and what to do, then bang! We wing it; they shoot it."

"Nervy," Jack said.

"Crazy is more like it," Miranda said. "I'd better go get in costume. Let's meet back here, okay?"

Her costume was coolness itself on a hot day—a knee-length tunic of pleated chiffon and a wreath of artificial flowers tied around her hair—but so disguised was she by the walnut-colored makeup smeared thickly over her arms, legs, hands, and face that she walked right up to Bobby and Jack and said hello twice before they recognized her.

"Get a load of you!" Bobby hooted. "Tar Baby Gaines."

"That's a perfectly disgusting thing to say," she retorted. "Not to mention if Auntie heard you making tar-baby jokes she'd tan your hide. And you two look just as peculiar—well, not Jack. He just looks like his usual Apache."

"That's me all over." Jack sighed, gazing down at the dark expanse of leg showing under his white cotton tunic. "Just once in this cockamamy game I'd like to get into a bath at night without the water turnin' brown. It'd make a lot more sense if they just went out and got real Indians."

Bobby glanced over Miranda's head to where the Denishawn dance corps was stretching and posing at the base of the grand staircase. "Hadn't you better get over there and learn the choreography?" he said mildly.

"I just wanted to make sure..." She paused awkwardly.

159

"We'll be right here, at the side of the steps," Jack said reassuringly. "Go on, squirt."

Miranda was shown to her place on the top rise of the wide steps by a harried assistant. The girl next to her, in a short tunic like Miranda's but with ribbons wound around her muscled dancer's legs, was flexing her feet and marking arm movements with the distracted frown of someone trying to remember something terribly important.

"Excuse me," Miranda said tentatively when the girl paused to massage her calf. "Can you show me the steps?"

A blank, blinking stare.

"I'm new."

The girl rolled her eyes. In a bored voice, she said, "Ok-a-a-ay. Start like this—" And she struck a pose with her feet flat, her legs bent at the knees, and her torso twisted to one side. "Turn sideways, flat like a board. Lift your arms with your elbows bent. Point your hands—look, like mine. Make 'em flat, like an Egyptian, see? Then, on the count of four—"

"Excuse me," Miranda said politely. "How do I know when to move?"

"There'll be someone screaming out counts," the girl said languidly. "Okay, you step down onto the next step—right foot, honey, right foot!—then back up, then down two, then back up one, always keeping your arms up and your head in profile. And one, and two, and three, and four.... Not bad. Anyway, we do that four times, real slow, and then we do spinning turns, a half turn on each count. Four times. We'll run through it before they shoot. You got it?"

Miranda nodded unhappily. "I think so."

Turning had never been Miranda's strong suit. Leaping was different. She could leap like a gazelle, higher and farther than anyone else in the class held every week in the basement of the Leewood Heights Second Methodist Church, but turning was sheer torture. Her teacher, a world-weary Russian of indeterminate age whose white face powder and mauve rouge always made Miranda think of a Toulouse-Lautrec poster, had finally given up and allowed as how young Miss Gaines had started ballet too late in life to ever attain "de pr-r-r-oper pirouette," that terrifying combination of abandon and control.

And so when Miranda, led by her sullen companion and feverishly whispering the beats to herself, launched into the formalized spinning turns, it was inevitable that she would try too hard, spin too fast, and lose control. Spinning dizzily from foot to foot, Miranda somehow managed to smack the girl in the chin with an outflung arm, who then lost *her* balance and stumbled off the top step into two other dancers, who then lurched forward into another knot of dancers, and so on and so on. Like a snaking line of dominoes felled by the touch of a single finger, the Denishawn dancers stumbled and reeled and lurched downward into a tangled, yelping mass of greasepainted legs and chiffon and silk ribbons at the bottom of the steps, cursing and shrieking and owlishly squawking, "Who? What? Who? Ow!"

Miranda was left halfway up the steps, gasping, her lovely flower wreath tipped drunkenly over one eye. She lay across the steps, legs sprawled in front of her, and leaned back on her elbows, chin slumped to her chest. *I've done it this time,* she thought miserably.

Then, as in a daydream, she heard the resonant voice from the night shoot boom out, "Ga-a-a-ad! Trouble in paradise so soon?" As though a fox were moving invisibly through a field, a path parted in the crowd, and Miranda heard sibilant whispers and hissing as the dancers and the extras began shushing each other. An uneasy silence fell, and the shallow wooden risers beneath her shook as someone strode up them two and three at a time.

Slowly, she lifted her eyes. Beautifully polished shoes...improbably long legs...tweed trousers bagged at the knees from long hours in the director's chair... vest with watch fob, finely tailored Norfolk jacket, shirt laundered to a snow-blind glare, silk tie firmly knotted. The sun was behind him, and she saw his face as a dark shape topped with a peculiar-looking mushroom of a hat with the crown cut out. She narrowed her eyes against the harsh backlighting, and the features came into focus: a large noble head, narrow boned and long jawed, with an imposing beak of a nose. Deep-set gray-blue eyes, heavy-lidded and hooded like a bird of prey. The mouth was long and mobile, and generous.

There he was, the man she had seen on the stage of Clune's Auditorium and in a hundred newspapers and back issues of *Moving Picture World*. The man C.J. referred to in hushed tones as The Master. The man who made actresses into gauzy paragons of wounded virtue, the man whose skill and imagination she had seen cause grizzled veterans and cynical know-it-alls to weep like children, the man with whom many said the moving picture game began—and ended. David Wark Griffith.

He was looking down at her—not angrily, or even unkindly—but definitely waiting for an explanation.

An oddly fatalistic calm came over Miranda, and she said the first thing that came into her head. "Where are you from?"

"Kentucky" was the startled reply.

"My mother was from Georgia."

"Ah-hah! A Daughter of the South!"

"I'm a half-breed, actually," Miranda said, leaning back on her elbows and squinting up at him. "My father was from New Jersey."

"Well, if ya'll don't tell anyone," he said, thickening his accent for effect, "I won't, either. I gather you are responsible for this minor catastrophe."

"Yes, sir," she said. "I'm sorry, sir. I got carried away, and they just went over." She spread her hands helplessly. "Like dominoes."

"I know," Griffith said. "I saw. From the platform." A chuckle started low in his throat and built into a great delighted rolling burst of basso laughter.

Miranda got to her feet and shoved her wreath back up onto her forehead. "My friend Bobby once told me I go through life with one foot on a banana peel and the other in my mouth," she said, and started down the steps.

"Just where do you think you're going?"

"Home."

"Oh, no," said Griffith. "It's a lo-o-ong way to the front gate. Who knows what deviltry you could incite between here and there? No, dear child, you come with me." He put a hand under her elbow and escorted her down the steps and across the great plaza, and the people made way for them in true biblical fashion. Miranda darted a look over her shoulder and saw Bobby and Jack staring after them with their mouths open.

"Ever see anything like that?" Griffith asked her. He was pointing to a 115-foot-high two-level platform that had been mounted on a railroad flatcar and set on narrow-gauge tracks, and that was balanced and counterbalanced so sensitively that it could be pushed along as smoothly as cream flowing from a pitcher.

"I've never seen anything like *anything* you've got around here," Miranda said breathlessly.

"Had an elevator built in," he said. "That's what we're doing this morning. We'll start at the top and descend while we go along the rails to the dead stops, over there. If all goes as I expect, it'll look like we're floating down into the very heart of the city itself. Well, come along."

Miranda stared dumbly at him.

"Up, child," he said with a grin. "Stay very still and very quiet, and you'll see something you can tell your grandchildren about one day."

They rode up to the top of the tower, the ten-foot-square platform crowded with Griffith, a few guests allowed the honor and privilege of witnessing the great tracking shot from the eagle's nest, and two Pathé cameras. One was manned by Billy Bitzer, stolid, thick-set, and uncommunicative. At the other was a round-faced boy with lank, straw-colored hair that kept falling in his eyes. *Why, he's not much older than I am,* Miranda thought, *and he's every bit as excited. He's just better at hiding it.*

One of the guests was a short, athletically built man who kept bouncing soundlessly on the balls of his feet, gazing around him with childlike enjoyment and occasionally flashing a dazzling, infectious grin. His teeth were very white against his tanned skin and sleek dark hair, and he looked strangely familiar. Miranda stared at him covertly for a minute or two, then realized, with an ecstatic catch of breath, that she was no more than three feet away from Douglas Fairbanks, the greatest swashbuckling matinee idol of them all!

The gunshot signals came, and they began to make the descent in tense excited silence broken only by Griffith's occasional murmured comments to Bitzer and the rhythmic metallic grinding of the cameras. Down and in they went, sinking weightlessly into the heart of light and shadow and movement and color, floating over the Denishawn dancers who were posturing angularly on the steps, drifting past the crowded balconies and rearing elephants and the three bands trumpeting with clarion brightness the eminence of Bel, descending ever-lower to the long banquet table with the King at one end and his Princess Beloved at the other, bound together by two white doves pulling a miniature golden chariot wherein lay a white rose. Down they went until the dead stops halted the platform and everyone let out their breath in one relieved, thrilled rush.

As the self-congratulatory backslapping and hollering burst like water from a dam on "Cut," Miranda slipped off the platform and went around to the back, welcoming the shade. Heat waves and dust eddied at her feet. She was dazed and light-headed and filled with a deep, wordless satisfaction.

There Griffith found her a few minutes later, leaning up against the platform struts. He took her chin between thumb and forefinger and tilted her head up to the sun. Miranda could feel him vibrating like a softly tapped drum, swept up in the rare moment in an artist's life when everything comes together to make not just the whole, but a new and greater vision than first imagined.

"Well, Daughter of the South?" he said softly.

"Thank you," she whispered.

Gently, he turned her head to one side, then the other, studying her dispassionately. As Miranda's eyes met his, she sensed he was seeing her for the first time as a composition of light and shadow, not just an amusing diversion of the moment. After a long moment he released her and stood, grinding his fists into the small of his back with a faint groan. Miranda waited, staring up at him.

"Good bones," he announced. "*Very* good eyes. We're not casting anything but extras through the end of the picture, but come see me in the spring when this foolishness wraps."

"Will you . . . ?"

"Yes?"

"Will you remember me?"

"Will I remember you," he said, gazing over her head. "Will I remember you. Will I remember the

166

Daughter of the South who came perilously close to bringing the most ambitious and complicated shot in the history of this young and noble art to a crashing halt?"

He paused dramatically, one hand placed over his heart, and Miranda found herself thinking that C.J. had copied more from this man than how to construct a scenario or frame a shot.

D. W. Griffith looked down at her, the corners of his hooded eyes crinkling with amusement. "Oh, I'll remember you."

Miranda drifted away on winged feet to the edge of the crowd, where Bobby and Jack were waiting for her. The expression on their faces could only be described as naked, consuming envy. She was unaccountably red-faced, however, and answered their excited questions on the walk home with distracted monosyllables. They were halfway down Talmadge with the Gaines bungalow in sight when she realized the root of her shame, and she stopped and stared thunderstruck at them. "I never even said a word about you," she said in a broken whisper. "I was just thinking about myself." Her voice trailed away, and she blushed with embarrassment.

"Serves us right for deserting you," said Jack.

"You did, didn't you? I looked around and you were gone."

"We just didn't know what to do, Randa. By the time we got over to you, Mr. Griffith was there and, well—"

"I'll tell you what it means, Red," Bobby said.

"Jumping at your chance? Thinking only of yourself?" He flashed her a lopsided grin and punched her shoulder. "Means you're a real actress after all."

They toiled in the vineyards of Old Babylon until the end of that week before returning to the painted cow towns and painted ponies of Inceville, and although Miranda searched in vain for the mushroom hat bobbing above the three thousand extras swirling about the vast set, she did not again encounter the charismatic Mr. Griffith.

On the sunny morning that was their last, Miranda and Bobby and Jack had, with some judicious elbowing, jockeyed themselves into the front row of extras, hoping to show on the mighty silversheet as more than Babylonian dots. A man approached them from out of the milling crowd, and five minutes later Miranda had another piece of the sad puzzle that was Bobby's past.

The man was perhaps fifty, but looked much older. It was not so much the unflattering makeup or the stark cruelty of the sun as the loose skin around his eyes and at the base of his throat. Perhaps it was simply the way he held himself like an abused dog waiting for the next blow. He shuffled over to them and stopped in front of Bobby. Underlying the expected odor of greasepaint and uncleaned costume was the sour reek of too many years of too many late nights and too much alcohol.

"Hey!" the man said to Bobby. "It is you. Marie Gilmerry's li'l by-blow. How ya doin', kiddo?"

The blood drained from Bobby's face. "I'm sorry,"

he said stiffly. "You must have me confused with someone else."

"Say, what gives?" said the man. "We played together. Back in '10, or maybe it was '11. Des Moines.
Don'cha remember?" He stared at Bobby's rigid face
and his expression sharpened with comprehension. "I
could have sworn...," he said slowly. "Sorry. My mistake. Beg pardon." He sketched a ragged salute and
wheeled back into the crowd.

Jack retied the lacings on his tunic with studied
deliberation. Miranda turned her attention to a ragged
bit of cuticle on her thumb. Bobby fixed on the distant
hills.

"I knew him," he said after a minute.

"Then why—," Miranda started to say, and Jack
laid his hand on her arm.

"Gilmerry?" he said casually.

"My name," Bobby answered, his eyes on the horizon. "Before I changed it. You have to swear you'll
never breathe a word of this. Not to a living soul."

"We won't," Miranda said.

"You don't have to tell us," Jack said kindly.

Bobby looked at them for a long, hard minute,
then, as though he had reached some sort of a decision, shrugged and looked away. "After my mother
died, I was supposed to go to a state home. Orphanage.
So I cut out. I don't suppose anybody's still looking for
one kid who fell through a crack, but— I guess you
could say I'm used to keeping one eye over my shoulder." He ran a hand through his hair and grinned
weakly at them. "I'd better go put the old boy straight.
He didn't look so good."

"Demon rum's got that man by the collar," said Jack.

"Him and half the actors I ever knew," Bobby said bitterly. "Something about the life makes 'em crawl right into the bottle and pull the stopper in after. Poor Bennett."

"Bennett?" said Miranda.

"Bennett Allardyce Fosdyke. Jeez, how'd I remember that? About as talented an actor as C.J."

"Oh, the poor man," said Miranda.

"Back in a minute," Bobby said, and walked off.

Miranda waited until he was well out of earshot. "Jack? What's a by-blow?"

"Someone born on the wrong side of the blanket," he said carefully. "It means your parents weren't married."

"I should have guessed," she said in a stunned voice.

"It ain't exactly the worst thing in the world," Jack said equably, "unless you think it is. Does explain his tight mouth some. That boy's a real case of down to Gehenna."

"What?"

"It's a line from a poem. Kipling, if I remember rightly. 'Down to Gehenna or up to the Throne—'"

"'He travels the fastest who travels alone,'" Miranda finished. "I can't believe you said that. He's got that written on a scrap of paper that he keeps taped to the mirror in his makeup box."

"Fits the profile," Jack said thoughtfully. "The way he always acts like nothin' means a darn thing."

"He cares about his work," Miranda said.

"That ain't what I meant, honey. I mean the way he acts like you don't matter to him, or Miss Lucy, or that crazy C.J. He's been dealt some bad blows along the way, and I guess he decided to play it close to the vest."

Miranda looked up at him, and her eyes filled with tears. "He does care about us, doesn't he?"

"Of course he does." He smiled down at her. "Listen, Miranda-mouth, I'd just as soon you don't tell him we talked about this."

"Never," she whispered. "Never in a million years."

A Stiff Price to Pay

I declare," Lucy said, her voice sharp with exasperation. "That man would be late to his own funeral."

"I've never understood that," said Miranda. "Why would anyone want to be on time to their funeral?"

It was Thanksgiving Day, and they had been hard at it since sunup. The little bungalow was tidy, gleaming, and redolent of the mouthwatering, stomach-rumbling aroma of roasting turkey and cornbread dressing and the spicy fragrance of cranberries simmering on the back of the big black stove, and mince and pumpkin pies cooling on the larder windowsill. They were standing in the dining room with Bobby and Jack, who had accomplished much of the housework (Jack willingly, Bobby under threats of bread and water) while Lucy and Miranda had made alternate chaos and order of the kitchen. Everything was now done. The Donnellys and Zeb and Mrs. Norwood had arrived—on time and dressed in their Sunday best—and were chatting amicably in the parlor. The dining-room table was set with Grandmother Gaines's Haviland

Limoges with the tiny pink-and-gold roses, and all the silver serving pieces and curious spoons and pickle forks Miranda hated to polish. The damask tablecloth glistened with starch and ironing, the napkins were folded cunningly into pleated fans and placed dead center on the service plates. Celery and olives and fancy pickles were arranged in the cut-glass relish dish. The salt cellars were filled. The great platter waited to receive, and Jack had stropped the big bone-handled carving knife to a fine edge. There remained only for Miranda to light the candles and Lucy to call everyone to the table. But where, oh where, was C.J.?

"Maybe he's bringing some dailies," Jack said helpfully. "And he had to go out to the studio to pick them up."

"We have had enough of that, thank you very much," Lucy said sourly. "This is Thanksgiving, after all."

Although C.J. had become established solidly on the Kay-Bee roster of directors, he still worked the way he always had: as far from prying eyes as possible. In his search for a private screening room, he had settled on the long central hallway of the Talmadge Street house. He had wheedled Lucy and Mary into mounting a six- by six-foot mirror at the far end, supposedly to help the dressmaking business but in truth because it was the finest surface on which to show film, crisp and silvery and magical. Over the last few months he had arrived every night after dinner with a fresh can of dailies and a notepad, working long after everyone had gone to bed. (Miranda, Lucy, and Bobby kept earplugs in their nightstands to drown out the ratchety whir of the projector, which lived in the coat closet during the day.) There he would be, night after night, muttering and pacing and filling the ashtrays—accompanied, oddly enough, by Mrs. Norwood, whose priceless acerbic comments he first found amusing, then came to trust.

"A Thanksgiving surprise, he said," Lucy grumbled. "'Set two extra places, Lucinda, My Sweet, I'm bringing a surprise.' I hope you got that knife good and sharp, Jack. I have had just about all I can take of that man and his surprises."

"Doorbell," Bobby announced. "Stay here, Miss Lucy. You, too," he said to Miranda. "I'll get it."

"You know what it is, don't you?" she said.

He cocked a finger at her and strode quickly from the room. They heard the front door bang open, then a startled cry from Mary Donnelly.

"Have I got a Little Sister around here somewhere?" trilled a sweet soprano voice.

"Dulcie!" Miranda shrieked.

A petite blond girl with a heart-shaped face dashed into the dining room and threw her arms around Miranda. "Oh, sweetie, let me look at you," she cried, and pulled back to hold Miranda at arm's length. "Goodness, you've grown a foot!"

"You haven't," Miranda giggled. "What are you doing here? I was beginning to think I'd never see you again."

"One of Charlie's mysterious telegrams," she said, smiling impishly. "'Delicious, the hour has arrived! The time is now!' You know."

"Do we ever," Lucy said, coming over to kiss Dul-

cie's cheek. "This is delightful! It's wonderful to see—"
She looked over Dulcie's head and caught sight of the
group clustered in the front hall beside two bulging
suitcases and a precarious stack of hatboxes. "Oh,
dear," she murmured, and squared her shoulders res-
olutely. She walked around Miranda and Dulcie and
went toward a tall, rawboned woman dressed in full-
blown Victorian mourning—a dismal display of rusty
black silk and jet beading topped by a hideous hat
with a knee-length veil—and extended her hand.

"My dear Mrs. McGill," Lucy said graciously.
"How lovely to see you again. Welcome to California."
Her gaze met C.J.'s, and he grimaced and rolled his
eyes. "Do come in. You remember Miranda."

Miranda's heart had dropped to her shoe tops the
moment she spotted The Widow. "All the charm of
Caligula, all the grace of a McCormick reaper" was
one of the phrases C.J. used to describe Dulcie's
mother, and for once his fulsome style was on the
mark. Of the late Mr. McGill little was known and less
was said, but it was generally assumed the poor man
had died simply to get away from her. The Widow was
simply *awful*. And she was trouble.

Charles James Tourneur had fallen in love with
Dulcinea Josephine McGill the first time he clapped
eyes on her at the old Biograph studio in New York,
and she with him. They were an odd match but an excellent one. Dulcie's innate goodness and accepting
nature smoothed the peaks and valleys of C.J.'s tem-
perament, and his drive and energy galvanized her
small flowery talent into performances of limpid,
heartbreaking beauty. There was only one problem,

however: the difference in their ages. This bothered neither C.J. nor Dulcie, but it was a neurotic fixation with The Widow, who, because Dulcie was not yet twenty-one, held legal sway over the girl. The situation had reached a cataclysmic, screeching boiling point the summer before when, in a last desperate attempt to wean Dulcie away from "that disgusting little man," The Widow had called The Motion Picture Patents Company down on the struggling independent filmmaker in the hope of smashing C.J.'s dream forever. Only the frantic efforts of everyone, including Lucy and The Pine Street Irregulars, had pulled the baby from the fire. An uneasy truce had been negotiated between C.J. and The Widow—but only after Dulcie, who had been supporting her mother since she was ten, threatened to leave Mamma to her own devices and finances once and for all.

"How do you do, Mrs. McGill," Miranda said sullenly. Lucy cleared her throat pointedly, and Miranda forced a smile and a curtsey.

The Widow glared stonily at her without replying, then turned abruptly to Lucy and said, "I need to freshen up."

"Certainly, dear, come right this way." Lucy put her hand under The Widow's elbow and led her away, determinedly keeping up a one-sided flow of pleasant chatter.

"It's been a long day," Dulcie said awkwardly. "She's tired from the trip."

"Oh, gosh," Miranda blurted, and turned to Jack, who was standing by the window attempting to blend his six feet plus into the background. "Dulce, this is Jack Bell. Jack, this is Dulcie McGill."

"Pleased to meet you, Miss McGill," said Jack, and walked toward her with his hand out. "Randa here talks about you all the time."

"I've certainly heard about *you*," Dulcie said, dimpling prettily as she placed her tiny gloved hand in his big sun-browned paw. "You're a real honest-to-goodness cowboy, aren't you?"

"Sort of . . . I guess," he said, and blushed.

"Then come and tell me all about it. I'm dying to learn how to be a real westerner," she said, and began to draw him across the hall. Jack stumbled on the rug and recovered clumsily, and Miranda began to giggle again as she watched them go into the parlor. A *westerner?* she thought fondly, looking at Dulcie's cascading sausage curls, the sheer hat trimmed with silk peonies and moiré ribbons, the dainty blue taffeta traveling suit and Chantilly lace blouse, the embroidered silk hose and size-four French-heeled satin slippers. Dulcie McGill on horseback in dusty denim and bump-toed boots? *That's about as likely,* she thought, *as Jack Bell in white tie and dancing pumps.*

Bobby strolled into the room with his hands in his pockets and a sly grin on his face. "You're missin' all the fun," he said. "Somebody ought to tell Jack that Dulce's the worst flirt in town and it doesn't mean a thing. Poor fellow's gone all red and dithery."

"You knew she was coming and you never said a word! I could kill you where you stand!"

"Don't get sore, Red. The Boss made me promise.

He didn't even tell Jer'. Besides, it was worth it to see the look on your face."

"You are forgiven," Miranda said with a wave of her hand. "It's just too bad she comes with that, that *thing* attached to her."

"The Lord giveth and the Lord taketh away," Bobby said with a resigned shrug. "Although I still say it's an awfully stiff price to pay for getting Dulce back."

"Well, she better just leave us all alone," Miranda said angrily. "When I think of what she put us through last summer! We've done a pretty good job of convincing Auntie that Hollywood is a normal town after all, but if The Widow starts stirring up the pot with all her shenanigans—"

"You don't have to tell me what kind of trouble she can cause," Bobby said sourly. "She'll make Dulce miserable, and that'll get C.J. all riled up, and then everything goes out the window and we're stuck in a two-reel weeper. Jeez!"

"Maybe she learned her lesson last summer." Miranda sighed. "Maybe this time she'll behave."

"Yeah? Two bits says you're dreamin'."

"Don't take it, Missy," C.J. said from the doorway. "It's a sucker bet."

Miranda looked at C.J. and saw that his face was flushed, his eyes glittering with excitement. "What *is* Dulcie doing here?" she asked.

He raised his hand and smiled mysteriously. "Later, Rat Girl. All will be revealed in the fullness of time."

Dinner was ended, the guests sprawled replete and happy around the wreck of Lucy's lovely table like so much flotsam beached by the tide. C.J. leaned back and surreptitiously undid a few buttons under the guise of fiddling with his watch.

"I ... am ... going ... to ... die," Miranda announced.

"You sure can pack it away for a little bit," Mrs. Norwood said admiringly.

"This little piggy went to market, this little piggy—," said Bobby.

"Three pieces of pie?" she retorted. "I only had two."

C.J. picked up a knife and rapped the side of a wineglass.

"Not the Waterford!" Lucy yelped.

C.J. pushed back his chair, stood, and spread open his jacket to hook his thumbs into the armholes of his vest. "Dear friends and beloved colleagues," he began. "It is most appropriate that we gather together on this day of thankfulness—"

"Oy veh," Bobby moaned. "A speech?"

"Hush, lad," said Jerry. "Can't you see the man's got somethin' to say?"

"Thank you, Donnelly." C.J.'s round blue eyes panned over their upturned faces, allowing the moment to build. "A summer spent herding recalcitrant cowpokes up and down the barren slopes of Santa Ynez Canyon has paid off handsomely, my friends," he said, and smiled contentedly. "No more shall my hands be bound by the rusty shackles of the two-reeler. No more! That splendid judge of talent and character known to you all as Mr. Thomas Ince has seen the light and handed me the plum of all plums. A feature-length saga to be shot on location in the

179

Sierras, which I shall have the pleasurable responsibility of casting and—"

"Hot dog!" Bobby cried, and tossed his napkin into the air.

Miranda's heart began to thump. *It's going to happen,* she thought. *We're going to be together again, the way I wanted from the very first moment I met them.*

"Just tell me I don't got to be a bartender no more," Jerry said excitedly.

"You don't," said C.J.

"Praise be," Jerry said. "I'm comin', Baby."

"Who's Baby?" Jack whispered to Miranda.

"Jerry's camera," she whispered back. "It's a Pathé—"

"There is, however," C.J. said loudly, "one rather sizable fly in the ointment."

"Ain't there always?" said Jerry.

"You had better not mean *me,*" The Widow said ominously.

"Madam, please," C.J. said, laying a hand over his heart. "Water over the bridge, I assure you. The past is as dead as the late lamented dodo. No," he said grimly. "I was referring to that Brooks Brothers nightmare—"

"Sully?" Bobby said. "Oh brother."

"Why does he have to come along?" Miranda asked. "He'll spoil everything."

"Not if I can help it," C.J. answered. "He's been assigned to the picture, as my assistant and location scout."

"That fop?" Bobby snorted. "He couldn't scout cactus in the desert."

"It's my contention Ince wants the useless creature out of his hair," C.J. said morosely. "Call it the price of artistic freedom."

"Lots of abandoned mine shafts up there," Jack said mildly. "Any number of things could happen to a man didn't know the territory."

"Jackie, me boy, I think I'm going to like working with you. Speaking of which—," C.J. said, and fished around in his pockets until he came up with a grubby piece of lined paper folded in four and the stub of a pencil. He whipped the paper open with a flourish and looked around the table over the top of it, his eyes dancing with enjoyment.

"Got the bit in his teeth now," Jerry said cheerfully.

Mary and Lucy looked at each other and began to laugh.

"Silence, peasants!" C.J. said imperiously. "The epic under discussion is *Brothers of the Trail*. To be directed, need I say it, by Charles J. Turner—"

"You're not French anymore?" Miranda interrupted.

"The great American oater directed by a Frenchman?" he said, and grinned disarmingly at her. "No, child, I have decided to return to my heritage, the soil of my roots—"

"Whatever they are," Bobby said.

"As I was about to say before I was so precipitously—and rudely—interrupted, the title is a tad pedestrian but we can always change it. It's a magnificent scenario, if I do say so myself. Bloodlust, romance, a barroom brawl to end 'em all, and enough snow to satisfy the Czar of all the Russias. It'll play a treat. Now let me see...." He gnawed on his pencil. "Jerry

181

on Baby: That goes without saying. Calhoun, I'd like you to set the stunts and the fight scenes. Ince says he'll spare you if you want to sign on. How about it, old man?"

Zeb dared a glance at Lucy, who was whispering with Mary, her blond hair shining in the candlelight. "Depends," he said tersely.

"I'll take that as a conditional acceptance," C.J. said, making a tick on his list. "Jack?"

"Yes, sir?"

"Like to play a lead?"

Jack swallowed. "I don't think so."

"Excellent! A humble actor is a treasure above rubies. You have toiled in the dreary vineyards of Inceville long enough—as haven't we all?—and it's time we got you out from under all that furniture polish and feathers. You will do very nicely as Ben Dillard, the hero. And you'll look well with Dulcinea, who will, *naturellement*, 'personate the heroine with her customary flair and delicacy. Ah, to have My Pet before my camera once again. What rapturous delights! What joy awaits! Roberto, I'm casting you against type—"

"Here it comes. Crepe hair and spirit gum. Up at the crack of dawn to get into makeup and—"

"Do credit me with *some* intuition," C.J. snapped. "No, deah boy, I am offering you a crack at Liam O'Grady, the villain. Evil, tormented, a thoroughly nasty piece of work. It'll be more fun than eating peanuts and no one will suspect a thing with that innocent mug of yours." He sat down again, drew his chair up to the table, and looked over at Bobby. "Interested?" he said, arching an eyebrow.

182

"Are you joking?" Bobby said eagerly. "A chance not to dig my toe in the rug and be winsome? I'll say!"

"Anything for me, Boss?" said Miranda.

"Anything for you. Hmm," C.J. chewed the end of his pencil and refused to meet her eyes. "Let me see." He spread the list open on the tablecloth and ran a forefinger down it. "What about—? No, no. I suppose you could play . . . Oh no, that would never do. Maybe I should see if Mae Marsh can— Ouch! No hitting the director. Oh, Ridiculous Child, would I go traipsing off into the godforsaken wilds without my dose of comedic relief? You shall play Roberto's sister, young Nellie O'Grady. A pivotal part, dead in the center of the action, and I trust you'll make it your own—you usually do."

"Wait a minute, Charles," Lucy interjected. "She is not—"

"Going anywhere without you," he finished. "Nor would I want her to. Can you arrange to cancel your lessons for a few weeks?"

"I suppose so," she said doubtfully. "There are always cancellations over the holidays, anyway."

"I'd like you to assist Mistress Donnelly with costumes and provide your terpsichorean talents. I understand there is a piano where we'll be staying, and nothing sets the mood for a scene like—"

"Just where exactly *are* we going?" Lucy said. "You've been rather vague on that point."

"Didn't I say? Sorry. Cullersville."

"Never heard of it," said Zeb.

"It's a mining town up near the Nevada border. Quite nauseatingly picturesque, or so I've been told.

183

There's a fine old hotel, saloons, stables, all the modern conveniences. Randall's arranged everything. Apparently the place is not very well known, but he managed to find someone with a survey map of the area. Which includes, sad to say," he said, with a nod to Jack, "the locations of the mine shafts, so there goes that idea." He consulted his list again, this time with an air of satisfaction. "Right," he said briskly. "That's done it. The *Brothers of the Trail* company is as follows: the Donnellys, the Gaineses, the McGills, Jack, Bobby and Zeb, Randall, and myself. This is not an expedition to darkest Africa so, please, all of you, one suitcase apiece. We'll use the natives if we need extras. Oh, and Donnelly—?"

"Yes, Boss?" Jerry said eagerly.

"I'm not about to lug developing equipment halfway up an Alp, so bring extra stock for Baby. We'll develop when we get back to town. I know it's dicey, but I'm willing to risk it. I've cleared it with Ince, so there won't be too much smoke and sulfur if we have to reshoot a few scenes. We're after exteriors, anyway. Mistress Mary?"

"Yes, Charles?" she said, a little warily.

"I'm allowing you one trunk for costumes. We'll go over the list later. Gingham and gun belts, the usual duds. A wedding dress for the girl, but that should be homemade looking. You'll be bored to tears, I'm afraid. Now, I'd like to be off by the tenth at the latest. I've planned a weeklong shoot, so we'll be back in plenty of time for Christmas."

"Christmas?" Mrs. Norwood broke in mournfully. "How'm I ever going to last to Christmas without my flickers?" She eyed C.J. coyly. "I don't suppose you'd have a nice little part for a character actress?"

"Now, now, Virginia," C.J. said fondly. "I have better plans for you, when we get back. You're my continuity girl, Precious. I couldn't finish a picture without you."

"That's more like it," she said, her wrinkled cheeks turning pink with the compliment. "Off you go, then. And bring me back a mountain man. Not too hairy. A nice bony widower with money under the mattress and no children!"

Amid the laughter and teasing that followed this remark, Miranda leaned over and whispered to C.J., "You did this on purpose, didn't you? So we could all be together again. So it could be like the old days, when we were...Oh, I've missed the Company. I didn't realize how much until this very moment."

C.J. leaned back in his chair, folded his hands behind his head, and smiled broadly at her. "What would be the point of going through the pluperfect hell that is picture making if you can't make your nearest and dearest suffer as well? Of course, I planned it. Call it Kay-Bee, call it Famous Players, call it Joe's Film Company. The banner under which we create is but a detail. The American Moving Picture Company is back in business!"

A Very Old Map

In 1915 Truckee was much the same as it had been for half a century: a small unremarkable town surrounded by perhaps the most spectacular scenery in all of northern California. There were great silent forests of fir and pine and hemlock, dramatic ravines through which sped icy, dark rivers, and there was Truckee Lake, a wide, still oval with the Sierras looming behind it like a vast painted backdrop. Within mere hours of downtown Los Angeles, in fact, lay lush tropical beaches worthy of Gauguin, coastline with the rugged severity of Maine's, rustic fishing villages with rustic inhabitants, foothills of sagebrush and saguaro, and deserts as bleak as the moon. In their never-ending quest for picturesque locations it was inevitable that, sooner or later, the moving picture folks down in Hollywood would discover Truckee—which may have explained why a town of such meager size boasted a large hotel and some two dozen saloons.

On a blistering cold afternoon in December, Charles J. Turner, director of the *Brothers of the Trail* company, and Miss Miranda Gaines, the juvenile lead of the company, strode out of the railway depot and surveyed the main street (indeed, the only street) of Truckee, which was a dismal welter of churned mud and frozen ruts. C.J. wore a fur-collared overcoat in which he resembled the manager of a disreputable opera company, a stylish homburg set at a rakish angle, and a large unlit cigar was clamped between his teeth.

"Ah, what ozone!" he cried, sucking the damp, frosty air into his lungs. "'A garden is a lovesome thing, God wot!'" he quoted obscurely. He stepped down off the sidewalk, then sprang back with an injured howl, shaking thick clots of mud off his brand-new Abercrombie & Fitch gum boots.

"I'm glad we're only staying the night," said Miranda, her voice muffled by the heavy wool scarf Lucy had insisted on winding around her head and halfway up her face. The Company was in the waiting room sorting out the luggage, but Miranda could not wait for her first glimpse of Truckee. She pulled down the scarf and whistled. "Just look at all those saloons. Auntie would never go for that!"

At that moment, a man in a ratty buffalo-fur coat came clomping along the board sidewalk.

"Aha!" C.J. exclaimed. "A native! Tell me, my good man, where can I hire transportation to the hotel?"

The man stared at him and spat a wad of tobacco juice to one side. "It's right across the street," he said laconically. "Most folks walk it."

The day had been a long one, the trip from Los Angeles via Sacramento seemingly interminable, and most of the Company went to bed directly after dinner. C.J.

and Jerry and Zeb stayed up late, planning and scheming over cups of cold coffee, while Sully went on a search for what he called "intellectual companionship and local color." Of the former he found no one who met his lofty standards. Of the latter he found more than he had bargained for, and when the Company gathered the following morning, Mr. Randall was sporting a lovely bruise over one eye and a split lip. When Miranda and Bobby and Jack came down to the lobby with their suitcases, Sully was slumped on a bench, his head tipped back against the wall. The Widow was bending over him, applying a compress to his manly forehead, and cooing and clucking with a maternal warmth that was quite out of character.

"So little culture," Sully said wanly. "So little finesse."

"What can you expect from a pack of lawless cowpokes?" they heard her say in a soothing tone.

Sully opened his eyes and caught sight of them. He smiled weakly up at The Widow. "Not in front of the children," he said in a low voice.

"Come on," Bobby said disgustedly. "Let's go get some breakfast before I lose my appetite completely."

"That's peculiar, those two cozying it up like that," Miranda whispered to him. "I'm not sure why, but it worries me."

"Aw, let 'em play with each other," Bobby replied. "Sully's harmless. As far as I'm concerned, it's a match made in heaven."

A night's sleep and a large breakfast will do wonders for even the weariest traveler, and as the narrow-gauge railway to the remote hamlets near the Nevada border wended its way up into the mountains, the Company's spirits rose with it. The snow lay heavy on the peaks above them and, softened by the bright winter sun, slid in fat marshmallow clumps from the pines as they passed, exploding onto the tracks in glittering powdery bursts. The air was very cold and grew thinner with each mile, but there was a dry tingling snap to it that made Miranda want to sing or dance or laugh out loud. When the whistle sounded on a steep switchback—a friendly, reedy toot not a bit like the low mournful wail of *The Limited*—she grabbed Bobby's arm and shrieked with sheer delight, and he grinned and shrieked right along with her.

Jack pulled his head in from the window. "We're coming in to Cullersville!" he announced. "I can see the sign, but I can't see the town yet."

The train pulled up the last rise and slowed to a stop, the engine chuffing billows of gray-white steam into the air.

"Come along, my chickens!" C.J. said, rubbing his hands together. "Grab your bags and meet your destiny!"

There was a man waiting on the patch of flat snowy ground that served as the Cullersville station. He was leaning against one of the posts supporting the splintery sign, his hands in his pockets, an ancient and overstuffed carpetbag at his feet. He was elderly and short and bowlegged, and wore an ankle-length sheepskin coat and a stained old Stetson that came down to his eyebrows.

C.J. sprang down from the train and strode over to the man with his hand out. "Delightful, delightful! The welcoming committee!"

"Name's Packer," the little man said, squinting up at him. "Who the deuce are you?"

"C.J. Tour—ah, Turner. Director of *Brothers of the Trail.*"

The man gave him a blank stare.

"The picture?"

A very blank stare.

"The picture company, man! We're here to shoot a moving picture."

"Well, I'll be hornswoggled. It warn't a gag after all."

"Come again?" said C.J.

The trainman, who served as conductor, engineer, and ticket taker on the remote line, leaned out of his window and waved his arm for attention. "Hey, Wilbur," he called out, pitching his voice over the hissing and metallic clankings of the engine. "You comin' or what?"

"Hold on," C.J. yelled over his shoulder. "Give us a minute."

"Make it snappy," the trainman yelled back. "I got a schedule to keep, such as it is."

C.J. turned to Mr. Packer. "You were wired, I believe."

"I was. Some duckbrain lookin' to rent my hotel for a week. A week!" he cackled. "I figured he was having me on."

"Having...you...on?" C.J. said through clenched teeth.

"A practical joke," he replied patiently. "I got a buddy down in Tahoe who's always sending me gag wires."

C.J. glared at him. "Just why is the idea of engaging your establishment so blasted amusing?"

"Got me a train to catch, sonny," said Mr. Packer. "Goin' down the mountain and I ain't a-comin' back till the daisies bloom. I allus do. Everyone knows *that*."

With admirable restraint, C.J. placed an arm around his shoulders and drew him a short way down the tracks. Snatches of conversation floated back to the Company, and it was clear from his oily tone and expansive gestures that The Boss was using every ounce of his considerable weight of persuasion. After a few minutes they turned and walked back to the train. C.J.'s expression was grim, Mr. Packer's positively beatific.

Jerry and Zeb and Jack had unloaded Baby and the costume and supply trunks, and Bobby and Miranda had lined all the suitcases up in a row. The assembled Company stood expectantly, their breath making clouds in the sharp air, the steam from the idling train swirling about their legs like ground fog.

"There seems to have been a minor lapse in communications," C.J. said to them. "Mr. Packer here was not prepared for our arrival. But everything is, ah, under control. Mr. Packer will go ahead and open the hotel for us, and we will follow with the bags. The trunks can stay until after we get something to eat and—"

"Mother of mercy!" Jerry exclaimed.

"What is it, Donnelly?" C.J. said wearily.

"I ain't leavin' Baby out here—she'll freeze to death."

Mary patted his arm. "You'd sleep with that thing if I let you."

"Whatever you think best," C.J. said curtly. He rubbed his forehead and frowned distractedly, then turned on his heel and walked to the front of the train. "Excuse me?" he called up. "If we wire a list of supplies down to Truckee, can you bring them up tomorrow?"

"Don't know when I'll be back this way," the man yelled down to him. "Line shuts down this time of year."

A vein started to beat in C.J.'s temple. "Call Mr. Thomas Ince at the Kay-Bee studios in Santa Monica," he snapped. "He'll pay whatever you ask."

"Special run'll cost ya" was the shouted reply.

"Whatever!" C.J. howled. "Whatever it takes!"

"It's your nickel," the man said. In a blast of smoke and steam and squealing wheels, the train moved on up the mountain.

"How did you convince Mr. Packer to stay?" Miranda asked C.J. as they were trudging along the narrow road that wound the short distance between the railroad tracks and the town.

"I didn't convince him," C.J. said bitterly, and made a motion like he was reaching into a breast pocket for his wallet. "George Washington convinced him. Abraham Lincoln convinced him. And, God help me, Andrew Jackson convinced him."

The road twisted around a stand of hemlock and over a slight rise and, suddenly, there was Cullersville.

They all stopped, rooted as one on a gasping intake of breath.

In the silence that followed, Miranda heard a cardinal singing somewhere overhead and the wind sighing through the pines and a faint rubbery squeak underfoot as her weight shifted on the packed snow.

"Oh, Boss," she said after a minute. "What are we going to do now?"

In the days when the cry of "Gold!" rang through the California hills, Cullersville had been a bustling mining town with a prosperous dry-goods store, a weekly newspaper, a branch office of Western Union, a bank, a dressmaker, a livery stable, a lumber mill to keep pace with the building boom, two churches (one Baptist, one Methodist), a lending library in the back of the feed store, a literary society that met every Wednesday night over the post office, a hotel with feather beds, Turkey carpets, a French chef imported all the way from New York City, and a large saloon and dance hall optimistically named The Lucky Greenback. Then the gold ran out.

Gradually, the citizens of Cullersville drifted away like dandelion silk on the breeze. The churches and the bank, the lumber mill and the stable, and the miners' little raw-pine cabins crawling up the hills behind the town stood empty, sagging with damp and neglect, pulled to the ground by storms and timber rot, reclaimed by creeper vines and the relentless march of the pines.

The proud false-front stores lining the main street had remained relatively intact, the hitching rails waiting for the horses that would never come, the window of Beauchamp's Emporium still advertising in faded letters a sale on genuine Paris *chapeaux* for the ladies. The hotel was still standing, an echoing shell where dust lay thick on the floors and the fancy gilt mirrors threw back watery reflections of faded plush curtains and peeling veneer. The Lucky Greenback was still there, but the long mahogany bar was silent, the small stage where girls in satin and fringe had kicked and flirted and sung to the clunky strains of the upright piano, deserted.

But Wilbur Packer loved Cullersville—or what was left of it—with the blind unreasonable passion of the Confederates for their lost dreams of glory and cotton. He was born in Cullersville and, by gum, he was going to die in Cullersville. And so he stayed. On his seventieth birthday he had allowed his daughter to convince him to spend winters with her down in Truckee, and he'd had a printer there do him up some "high-class" calling cards, which read, in elaborate script:

Wilbur Josephus Packer, Mayor of Cullersville, California
Justice of the Peace, Raconteur, & Proprietor of
The Packer House Hotel. Reasonable rates.

One glimpse of Cullersville and The Widow folded her arms and glared at C.J.—preparing, Miranda sensed, for a verbal assault of unprecedented nastiness. Then a curious thing happened. Sully laid a hand on her arm and whispered something in her ear. Her rawboned features softened, and she actually *smiled*. The sight of The Widow smiling was somehow more disturbing than her usual vinegar-and-brimstone demeanor, and Miranda shivered uneasily.

Bobby, however, began to laugh. "What the heck," he said cheerfully. "I always wanted to see a ghost town."

"See one, yes," Lucy said dryly. "Live in one?"

Slowly, C.J. turned and gazed at Sully. "Ah, Mr. Randall," he said evenly. "Our location scout. One question, sir, if you wouldn't mind. Just how did you hear about this place?"

Sully ran a finger under his collar. "Chap I met in Los Angeles one night," he said defensively. "He was an old trail hand, a real cowboy. Knew these mountains like the back of his hand, he said. He should, I guess. He came through here with the Donner party."

"The Donners?" said Zeb. "Have mercy."

"How 'bout that," Jack said pleasantly. "Was he real old, this fellow?"

"About my age," Sully said loftily. "Perhaps a little older. Why?"

Jack narrowed his eyes and smiled into space. "If I remember my history correctly—and I usually do: It was my favorite subject—the Donner party tried to cross the Sierras in 1846."

C.J. snorted. "How much that map set you back, Sully, me boy?"

"Twenty," he muttered.

"He sure saw you coming!" Bobby hooted.

"With the headlamps on," C.J. said acidly. "Twenty simoleons for a map."

"It got us here, didn't it?" Sully said.

"No, you overeducated twit, the railway got us here," C.J. said. "Now I understand why the station-master in Truckee acted as though I'd gone barmy

195

when I purchased the tickets. The Donner party, my foot. As if it was something to brag on."

"Why not?" asked Miranda.

"They were a famous group of settlers," Jack explained. "Famous for getting in trouble, that is. It's a pretty grisly story. They got trapped in these mountains when the snows came. They managed to build a couple of cabins on Truckee Lake and hunkered down there for the winter. But there was no way over the passes, no way to get supplies. When their grub ran out they starved and went crazy and . . . well, Randa, honey, there's no nice way to say it. They et each other."

Miranda's eyes widened. "Really?"

Jack nodded.

"Fear not, Little One. Should we run short of comestibles"—C.J. shot a pointed glance at his assistant director—"I have a prime candidate for the spit."

"Really, Charles," said Mary. "Talk about bad taste. Oh, heavens!" She gasped. "What *have* I said?"

"Never mind, never mind," C.J. said lightheartedly. "Look at it this way. The train'll be back in a few days. And in the meantime, just look at this place, will you? Now that is what I'd call photogenic!"

They assembled that night in the dust-sheeted parlor of the hotel (after a meal of tinned beans, soda crackers, and coffee that Zeb said took him back to his days on the trail) for C.J.'s florid and gesture-laden description of the scenario. It didn't sound all that unusual to Miranda—it sounded depressingly like the Westerns they had been shooting all summer—but she cooed and made excited noises with the others.

Ben Dillard and Liam O'Grady were two stalwart young men prospecting for gold in a small town in the mountains. At the beginning of the story the best of friends, but by the eighth reel the deadliest of enemies, their friendship and trust forever ruined by their rivalry for the hand and heart of Rose Jefferson, Our Heroine. Miranda was comic relief, but her loyalties would be divided between all the players, making for conflict, drama, and, happily, many scenes in which she would be featured. Zeb and Mr. Packer and C.J. himself would fill in as extras in the saloon scenes. Sully was assigned to comb the hills around Cullersville every day from dawn till dusk until he found a cabin with a southern exposure and a fieldstone hearth.

Mr. Packer, whose reluctance to stay had evaporated completely with the chance to make his debut "in them newfangled flickers," raised his bushy eyebrows at this last assignment. "I don't want to tell you your business, Turner," he said to C.J., "but they ain't no cabins with fancy fireplaces 'round these parts. Leastways not any I can recollect."

"Is that a fact?" C.J. said blandly. "Well, Randall, you'll just have to look extra hard, won't you? Pack a sandwich and stay the night."

The snow began a few hours before dawn. A few scattered flakes at first, drifting lazily over the Sierras like powdered sugar from a sifter, slowly covering the world with a thin, fine layer ... then gathering, thickening, the wind rising to a steady keening as the temperature dropped.

By sunrise Cullersville was blanketed with a foot of fresh, crisp white that glittered and sparkled in the winter sun. The Company trickled out of their dusty bedrooms and down the main staircase into the lobby, blankets and quilts wrapped around their shoulders, yawning sleepily and blinking against the glare streaming through the dusty windows.

"This is gonna monkey things up for sure," Bobby said to Miranda in a murmured aside. "But I guess even The Boss can't control the weather."

C.J., however, took one look at the expanse of white and began rubbing his hands together and pacing, a sure sign that he was planning to seize the opportunity and change the tenuously constructed plot. "A snowball fight for levity," he muttered to himself. "Then it turns ugly. The girls stand in horror as Liam and Ben face off— Ooh, yes. *Yes!* Figures in a white landscape, yes, yes. Superb!"

"Hell's bells and little catfish," Wilbur said, staring out the front window.

Miranda came to stand beside him. "Don't you like snow, Mr. Packer? I love it! I was so afraid I wouldn't get to see any this winter. That's the one disappointing thing about living in Los Angeles—it never snows, not at all. And it's so beautiful, don't you think?"

"It's purty enough," he said mournfully. "If'n you likes that sort of thing. I don't. And the train don't, neither."

"Trains can't get through the snow?"

"Some, yes," he replied tersely. "If'n the passes choke . . . aw, never you mind, doll. We'll be fine. Now, how you like your eggs?"

"Scrambled," she answered. "With cheese."

"Me, too," Wilbur cackled. "Too bad we ain't got any."

"You know, Bobby," she said to him as Wilbur disappeared in the direction of the kitchen, "I think we've found Mrs. Norwood's mountain man."

"Children, children!" C.J. called out. "Front and center. The day's assignments, if you please. Donnelly, have you done what we discussed?"

Jerry nodded with satisfaction. "Got 'em all fitted up last night. Little bitty oil lamps for Baby."

"Your camera?" Jack said curiously.

"Got to protect me darlin' Baby," Jerry answered. "Comes right down to it, she's the most important member of The American. You see, freezing temperatures'll make static ee-lectricity on the film, and it shows up as flashes of light when you develop it. Ruins it fer sure. So you rig oil lamps to the camera, with pipes runnin' through Baby's innards. Keeps her from freezin' up. Works down to 'bout zero. After that . . . ?" and he shook his head.

"It'll work," C.J. said stoutly. "My faith in you is absolute. We are going to be shooting mostly establishing shots today," he went on. "You know the drill, Donnelly. Atmosphere galore. Roberto and Jack trudging through the snow with their gear, shots of railings and roofs piled with the stuff, sun glittering on the pines. Missy, I want you following them, but the snow is too heavy for your dainty legs, so we'll have lots of drama as you struggle behind. You know what I want?"

"Yes, Boss," she said happily. "You want me all fragile and delicate."

He grinned. "I know, it's a stretch. Calhoun, you have a nice prairie look to your pan, so I'm pairing you with Miss Lucinda. A few shots of you clomping up and down the sidewalk. Ma and Pa Hayseed go window-shopping. The life of the town, in miniature. Okay?"

"I don't mind if Miss Lucy don't," he answered shyly.

"Why should I mind?" she said, and his lined cheeks flushed.

"Randall?" C.J. said.

"Yes, sir. Right here, sir," Sully said nervously. He had been attempting, since their arrival the previous day, to dissolve into the background, slipping around corners whenever he heard C.J.'s robust tones and speaking only when spoken to, which was seldom.

"Keep the log," C.J. said shortly.

"But that's a mug's job," Sully whined before he could stop himself. "I'm an assistan—"

"Precisely." C.J. cut him off. "You are my assistant, and those are your duties. Unless you'd rather slope off into the hills to look for cabins?"

"No, sir," he said sullenly. "I'll keep the log."

"What's about me, Charlie?" Dulcie asked.

"Work, dearest. Backbreaking toil. We shall see Rose at the pump, hauling water, chopping wood, banking the fire. All with your back to the camera, with a shawl over your head so we think you're some dreary old charwoman. Until Ben comes toward you and calls your name...you turn...and we see your exquisite visage for the first time, in close-up, the Madonna of the Snows—"

"Backlit?" Jerry said excitedly.

"Need you ask?" C.J.'s eyes were twinkling. "Beats the suds and soaks, eh, Donnelly?"

Jerry sighed happily.

"That's it," C.J. said crisply. "Mary has your costumes. Extra layers underneath, all of you. Mr. Packer has agreed to put up some Thermos bottles of java, so the inner man won't freeze even if the outer man does." He clapped his hands smartly. "We begin!"

Snow, Snow, Snow

The snow came again that night, and the winds picked up, rising in pitch and tempo to a banshee howl. This was not the pretty, glittering snow of Christmas cards, falling decoratively through lamplight to the strains of "O Little Town of Bethlehem." Fine, sleety pellets, mean-spirited and purposeful, whirled down onto the little town of Cullersville with the force of a runaway freight train, driving through cracked walls and under doors, piling in monstrous drifts at the end of the deserted streets. This was no ordinary snowstorm—this was a blizzard.

It was just past dawn when Miranda heard bells ringing. For a minute she thought she was back in Leewood Heights and it was time for Sunday school, then she realized it was the big copper cowbell Wilbur used to call them to meals, clanging over and over again. She looked across the room to Lucy, who had awoken with a start and was sitting bolt upright, her curlpapers standing out from her head in disarray.

"Mercy!" Lucy said, her eyes very round. "Listen to that!"

Their beds were shaking, the walls trembled with

each blast of icy wind, and over the urgent clanging of the bell they could hear snapping and groaning noises, like the rigging of a ship in rough seas.

"Wake up! Wake up!" a voice was screaming. "Everybody, now!"

Miranda jumped out of bed and ran down the hall to the top of the stairs. Wilbur was standing in the lobby, fully dressed. C.J. dashed out of his room, striped nightshirt flapping wildly about his legs.

"Great gods above, man!" he howled over the banister. "I was *asleep.*"

"Be packed and ready to leave in twenty minutes," Wilbur screeched up at him. "The roof ain't gonna hold. I been up all night checkin' her, and let me tell you—"

C.J. may have had his flaws, but he was swift to assess a situation and swift to action "Go, Missy!" he said to Miranda, shoving her in the direction of the room shared by Dulcie and The Widow. "One if by land, two if by sea!"

Fear of being buried alive will put a spring into just about anyone's step. The *Brothers of the Trail* company was dressed, packed, and assembled in the lobby in seventeen minutes by C.J.'s pocket watch.

"All present and accounted for," he announced. "I assume, Packer, that you've wired for our transportation?"

"Telegraph's out," Wilbur said. "Wires must've blew down."

"There is a telephone, I presume."

"Sure," said the little man. "You want to walk five miles down the mountain."

"Oh, lovely," C.J. groaned. "Cast adrift on the frozen wastes, struggling vainly toward the lights of civilization. They'll find our bodies come spring, huddled together like those poor souls at Pompeii."

"You theatrical types sure do get all worked up," Wilbur said. "We're movin' to The Lucky Greenback. The saloon next door," he explained. "She's rode out every blizzard since '86, and she'll ride out this one." He looked up and sighed sadly. "Allus meant to shore up that roof."

"A saloon?" said Miranda. "Where will we sleep?"

"There's a whole flob of little bitty bedrooms over there," he answered. "Up on the second floor."

"What kind of little bitty bedrooms?" Lucy said suspiciously.

"I reckon you'd call 'em cubicles," he said uncomfortably. "Got a bed and a mirror, mostly."

"A bawdy house!" The Widow shrieked. "You're going to put us up in a *bawdy house*."

"Lady, lady, lady," Wilbur said patiently. "Don't get your bustle in an uproar. They ain't been a loose woman on the premises since oughty-ought." A misty-eyed look came over his face. "Elsie, her name was," he said nostalgically. "No teeth to speak of and a face like a washboard, but brother! could she—" He pulled up short and looked down at Miranda, who was hanging on his every word. "Heh-heh," he cackled. "Backward, turn backward, O time, in thy flight."

"That will be quite enough of that, Mr. Packer," Lucy said firmly.

Miranda looked at the front window. It was well past daybreak now, but the sky had lightened only slightly. Ugly sheets of sleet and snow dashed against the windows and hammered fretfully against the door. "How far do we have to go?" she asked Mr. Packer.

"I told ye," he said. "Next door. I went out and strung a rope from here to there. Man can get lost between the barn and his own house in a storm like this."

Zeb nodded. "Happened to a feller I knew back in Wyoming," he said grimly. "He went out to feed the stock. We found him the next day, two feet from the door, froze up like an icicle."

"How do you like livin' in the Old West now, Red?" Bobby teased her. "Ain't this just peachy?"

The Lucky Greenback was solidly built—Wilbur had been right about that—but it was cold as the grave. There was only one fireplace, downstairs in the main room next to the stage. The bedrooms were dismal little chambers, and after a brief inspection, Lucy suggested a good way to conserve heat would be to sleep dormitory-style in the two largest bedrooms at the opposite ends of the long upper hall. The Company spent the better part of the morning moving beds into these two rooms, and piling quilts and moth-eaten blankets against the windows and door sills.

The kitchen behind the long mahogany bar had not been used in decades, but after considerable effort (which, at least, kept the blood moving through their veins) Mary and Lucy and Zeb were able to get the stove cleaned out and lighted. Not that there was much to cook. Wilbur had been allowing his supplies to dwindle in preparation for his yearly departure to Truckee. He and Jerry went back and forth on the rope lifeline between the saloon and the hotel all morning, ferrying the contents of cupboards and cellar, each time appearing at the back door half frozen, snow and ice caking their mustaches and eyebrows.

"The pump done friz," Wilbur announced after a perilous investigation around the back of the building, then sent Miranda and Bobby and Jack outside to fill buckets and washtubs with snow. Set to melt by the stove, they would provide water for drinking, cooking, and washing. Wilbur had also found a twenty-gallon drum of kerosene in the shed, more than enough fuel for the lamps and the portable generator Jerry had brought along to power the Cooper-Hewitt incandescent lights.

It snowed without letup all that day and into the night...and for a second day and night, and a third, and a fourth...and a fifth...and a sixth. Wood became a problem almost immediately. The stove was temperamental and ate like a starving actor in a boardinghouse. The big fieldstone fireplace at the end of the dance hall supplied the only heat for all of the first floor—unless they wanted to huddle around the stove in the dark, cheerless kitchen—and had to be kept going at all times. There were plenty of chairs around the gaming tables in the saloon half of the main room, however, and when those were gone the men chopped up the tables for firewood. The unused bedsteads, luckily, were pine and not brass, and Jerry and Jack spent one whole afternoon turning them into kindling, throwing the bits over the banister for Miranda and Bobby to pile up at the foot of the stairs. The stair railings were the next to go, and only Lucy's impassioned pleading kept the battered old upright piano from the flames. "I'll freeze to death before I kill a piano," she cried. "Even one as pitiful as this!"

They could, C.J. insisted, keep chipping away at *Brothers of the Trail*. He had reworked the scenario yet again, optimistically tailoring it to The Lucky Greenback interiors. "I always hated how hot the lights were," Miranda said to him. "Now I love 'em. Put me in lots of scenes, Boss."

"Pneumonia!"

"I'm not that cold, really," she reassured him.

"No, *listen*." He grabbed her by the arms and stared into her face. "Use what you've got, right? Remember all that stuff we shot the first day, with you trudging along after the boys through the snow?"

"Do I!" Miranda exclaimed. "I thought my feet would never thaw."

"So we follow up. Nellie comes down with pneumonia, and Liam blames Ben. Why? Oh, who knows why," he said impatiently. "It'll play, that's the main thing. They have an argument over your sickbed, then Rose comes in to nurse you, and..." He let loose her arms and gazed into space. "The bed, your face wan and small on the pillow. A kerosene lamp flickering on the table. You're ill, really ill. We think you're going to die, your sweet young life cut short—" He pulled out his handkerchief and blew his nose loudly. "Well, child?" he said, looking down at her. "Think you can pull off a scene Pickford would give her eyeteeth for?"

"Sounds to me like close-ups, Boss," she said with a wide, slow smile. "Lots and lots of lovely close-ups."

"Mother of pearl," he groaned. "What have I spawned?"

But after a satisfying afternoon of tragedy and re-criminations—during which Miranda snuggled happily under a pile of quilts, while Bobby and Jack and Dulcie had to eat snow before every take so their breath wouldn't show on film—even C.J. admitted they were too cold and distracted to concentrate and suspended filming for the duration of the storm.

It became harder and harder to fill the time. The books that Miranda and Bobby had packed were all read by the third day. C.J. did Shakespeare until they begged him to stop, Lucy and Mary recited the poetry they had learned in school, and Miranda recited "The Wreck of the *Hesperus*" four times. Jerry taught them all the Irish ballads his mother had taught him, and Zeb gave the boys dance lessons with Lucy struggling and complaining at the upright, which was so far out of tune it was difficult to distinguish one note from the next. By the fifth day tempers were short, and Lucy relented and allowed Miranda to play poker with the men.

On the seventh day—or was it the eighth, or the ninth?—the storm finally broke. A sullen sun pried its way through the clouds, which C.J. claimed was sufficient to shoot a few outdoor scenes. Bobby and Jack were sent onto the front porch, bundled in so many layers of clothing Zeb was heard to say that he'd never before tried to set a fight scene where the fellers couldn't move their arms.

"I'm gettin' awful tired of hittin' you, Jack," Bobby said as they headed out the door. "We ought to call this thing *Brothers of the Brawl*."

"Now, Missy," C.J. instructed Miranda. "While Liam and Ben are whaling the tar out of each other, I want you to watch the action through the window here. Donnelly will be shooting over your shoulder, so all three of you are in the frame. Bang your little hands on the glass, scream in frustration—"

"Ah, yes, I see," Sully interrupted, nodding sagely. "The perfect metaphor for the alienation between the innocence of the girl and the violent world of the men—"

"Metaphor, he says." C.J. clutched his head as if staving off a migraine. "It's well below zero out there! I'm simply trying to avoid ruining good stock with static scratches. Usable is what I'm after. Art, if it occurs, is a bonus. You blockhead."

Late that night, Miranda awoke to the deep and immediate certainty that the person she loved best in all the world was calling her name. For one sweet hazy moment she thought it was her mother, whose face she barely remembered, whose voice was lost to her. She lay quietly and allowed her senses to swim to the surface as she listened to Lucy breathing softly beside her. Then it sounded again. A faint cry, thin and piteous and insistent.

That's one benefit of sleeping in your clothes, apart from keeping warm, she thought as she eased herself from under the covers. *You can sneak out at the drop of the proverbial hat.*

As she tiptoed down the long hall past the empty bedrooms, she remembered, suddenly, her midnight ramble through *The Limited* and wondered if Grover Johnson was out there somewhere in the dark, crossing the reaches of Nebraska under a winter moon, working away at a hundred small tasks and humming hymns to lift the silence. *The middle of the night is the best time,* she thought. *Anything can happen.*

She was breathing through her mouth—it made less noise than your nose, which was apt to whistle—as she crept down the main staircase, nervously eyeing the chasm beyond the stairs where the railings had been.

A fingernail moon rode high in the trees, the frail light reflecting off the snow and casting silvery rectangles on the floor of the old saloon. As Miranda tiptoed across the floor, a shape disentangled itself from the shadows and rose against the windows.

"Who goes there?" came a husky whisper.

"Jack?"

"You heard it, too?"

"Woke me up," she whispered. "What is it?"

"Come here, I'll show you." She went to his side and he pointed out the window. "There," he whispered. "See? At the bottom of the steps."

Miranda followed his finger. "No, I . . . oh yes!"

He cracked the door and a gust of icy wind shot in. Miranda shivered and hugged herself. "Don't make any sudden moves," he said. "We don't want to frighten it."

They waded across the snow-covered porch to the steps. "Come on, honey," Jack breathed. "Don't run away now, baby, come on to Jack, sweetie. Come on now, come on." He pursed his lips and made soft kiss-

210

ing sounds. A small ragged shape slipped up the steps and crouched at his feet, and he bent down and gathered it into his arms.

"Got 'er," he whispered. "Quick, inside."

They slid back through the door and stood, shivering in a sliver of moonlight. Wordlessly, Jack led Miranda to the kitchen, the bundle in his arms making soft, plaintive cries. Miranda went to the table and fumbled around until she found a box of sulfur-tipped matches beside the kerosene lamp. Fingers shaking with cold and excitement, she struck a match, put sputtering flame to wick, and turned to see their prize.

"You hold it while I look for grub," Jack said—and placed in her arms the scrawniest, dirtiest cat she had ever seen. It pressed itself to her, digging its cold wet nose into the crook of her neck, frantic for contact and comfort and the life-giving warmth of another animal.

"Oh, the poor little thing, the poor little thing," Miranda crooned. She sat at the table in the circle of light, and the cat slid bonelessly to her lap and curled into a wet, shivering ball. Miranda put her hand out cautiously, expecting caution in return, a sniff of exploration, or even the recoil of fear. Instead the cat butted its head against her palm, rubbing against it frantically.

"Oh, you've done it now," Miranda whispered. She pulled up her skirts and made a nest, stroking and murmuring all the while. Gradually the shaking abated, and a face emerged: wide-set eyes, as green as grapes and flecked with turquoise, a delicately formed muzzle and chin, and the tangled remains of a magnificent ruff. Although it was caked with dust and dirt

211

and clumps of ice, its long coat snarled and lumpy with mats, Miranda knew that, once clean, the cat would be a pale apricot color patterned with orange.

"She's a marmalade tabby," she whispered excitedly. "My friend Carrie had one back home. She's beautiful."

"Powdered milk," Jack muttered to himself across the room. "Should be warm but I daren't light the stove. Oh, good, Uneeda biscuits." He broke the ice on the water bucket, mixed some milk in a pie tin, and tucked the box of crackers under his arm. "How's she doin'?" he said in a low voice as he pulled up a chair.

"She's so dirty," Miranda said. "I think her chin's white but I can't really tell—it's sort of a charcoal gray at the moment. She must be very old. Her backbone sticks up like a swaybacked horse."

"That's starvation," Jack said. "Been on her own for quite a few months by the look of it."

"What's she been living on?"

"Not much, I'd say. Scraps if she can find 'em, small critters. Mice after the grain in some of the old barns 'round here."

"The poor little thing," Miranda said again. "Who do you suppose she belongs to?"

"You, now."

"Don't you want her? You're the one who found her."

"Every girl should have a cat: It ought to be a law. Besides"—he smiled—"you match. Both redheads."

Miranda looked down at the creature, who returned a gaze of serene acceptance. "I always wanted a cat."

Jack crumbled a handful of crackers into the milk and mashed them into a semblance of porridge, then lifted the cat onto the table and set the pan beneath its chin. It emptied the plate rapidly and gratefully, then sat back and proceeded to wash. "Table manners!" he said delightedly. "That's a good sign, Randa. It means she's not wild, just abandoned. It also explains why she's so filthy. A cat on its own dare not clean itself too often—it has to be on the alert every second."

"We keep calling it a she. How do you know it's a her, I mean she's an it—" She stopped in confusion.

"Apart from the obvious, there's demeanor."

"It's almost a shame," Miranda said. "If she wasn't a she I'd name her Jack 'cause you rescued her."

"I had a wonderful dog when I was a kid, a Collie named Jake. A she-dog, too, and she didn't mind her name a bit. You could call her Jake. Short for Jacqueline, if you like."

"Jake?" Miranda said softly. "Oh, Jake?"

The cat lifted her head and stared at Miranda, her expression clearly stating: "Do you mind? I happen to be bathing!" She flicked a whisker, then twisted around to address a particularly grubby patch at the base of her tail.

Jack laughed. "Jake it is."

Lucy opened her eyes to the clanging of Wilbur's wake-up bell. "Good morning, darling," she murmured to Miranda. "Did you sleep well— Merciful heavens, what's *that?*"

"It's Jake," Miranda murmured, stroking the cat

curled up beside her. Jake buried her nose beneath a shaggy paw, as displeased with the coming of morning as her mistress.

"It's a cat!"

"Mm-hmm," Miranda said contentedly. "Mine."

"Well, I'm not sleeping with it," Lucy said crossly, flinging the covers aside. "In a box by the side of the bed if you must, and I'll not be responsible for feeding it, either." And she marched from the room, muttering, "A cat. Cats belong in the barn."

Miranda snuggled into Jake's soft orange fur, already much improved, and whispered, "Round one to us." She looked over at Dulcie, who was staring at them through her customary fringe of rag curlers. "Mornin', Dulce. Got me a kitty. Her name's Jake."

"Pretty" was the sleepy reply. "Tell you what. I'll make Charlie write her into the picture, then you can keep her for sure."

"Oh, Dulcie, you're a pal."

"Always wanted a kitty," Dulcie said, pulling the covers over her head. "Mamma wouldn't let me."

"Phooey on anyone who won't let you keep a cat. Right, Jake?" Jake blinked and stretched. "Right!"

'Ere I Meet My Maker

s it turned out, Jake's addition to *Brothers of the
Trail* was unavoidable. She trotted at Miranda's
heels like a dog, and, when not in her lap,
chose as her observation post the girl's shoulders, draped
from side to side with superb balance, tail switching,
green eyes scanning her new world.

"I played with an old character actress once who
wore a ratty fur scarf all the time," Bobby quipped. "If
you could train Jake to bite her tail . . . ?"

But Miranda was working off a lifetime of accumu-
lated cat hunger and brooked no insults. "She does *not*
look like an old fur piece," she replied hotly, tears
springing to her eyes. "She's *gorgeous*."

"Leave off, Bob," Jack spoke up. "The girl's in love."

"It's just a cat," Bobby grumbled.

"No such thing as 'just a cat,'" Jack said, pulling
him aside. "Nothing more fierce or possessive than the
love of a girl for her cat, which you'd know if you'd
had sisters like me. She's too old for dolls and too
young for babies. That fussing has to go somewhere."

"Uncle!" Bobby lifted his hands in surrender. "I still say it's awfully ratty looking," he added.

"Feeding and brushing and it'll come up a treat. You'll see."

"That's just it, Jack. The Widow did twenty minutes this morning on the milk she's giving it. We're out of flour and salt and real low on coffee. There's a shelf of canned goods left, but they're all rusty. I overheard Wilbur giving C.J. the lowdown this morning. We're skint. If we can't get out of here in the next day or two—or if someone can't get in—we're in for a bad time."

"Settle down, city boy," Jack replied. "We'll get out of here, one way or another. You're just not thinking about the situation as an advantage."

"Just what the heck is advantageous about this, I'd like to know."

"You and Randa still worried about Miss Lucy turnin' tail back to New Jersey?"

"Keep your voice down," Bobby hissed. "We're hoping she's forgotten."

"By the time we get back, she'll be too worn-out to even think of packing up the house," Jack said with a slow grin. "Leastways not right away. Don't worry if you don't absolutely have to, I always say. I was serious about Jake, though. Anything happens to her we might as well take Randa out back and shoot her. So I'll donate some of my rations." He folded his arms threateningly. "And so will you."

"Jeez! What a lot of fuss about a cat."

"I ain't talking about Jake. I'm talking about the

216

morale of this company, which is at this moment balanced on the head of a pin."

"You're right," Bobby said thoughtfully. "Count me
in, Jack."

"As long as we're on the subject, your little jokes
about the Donner party don't exactly help. Pinching
Miss Lucy's arm and yelling, 'Come and get it!'"

Bobby snickered. "You didn't like that?"

"No more than I like C.J.'s *Titanic* jokes when we
go rowboating in Griffith Park."

Wilbur stuck his head around the corner of the
kitchen door and waved the big copper cowbell up
and down. "Chow time!" he bawled. "Miz Donnelly's
bringin' it out."

The Company lined up along the bar—the only
place where they could all eat together since the
tables had been sacrificed—and smiled expectantly
at each other. Mary entered the room, a doubtful
expression on her face. She was carrying a large iron
kettle (wrapped in a towel to protect her hands from
the heat), which she set down on the bar.

Lucy entered with a stack of bowls on a tray. "Go
on, dear," she said to Mary. "It'll be fine."

Mary lifted the lid off the kettle. The steam rose
attractively—the smell that rose with it was something else again.

"What in the beloved name of Fanny Farmer *is*
that?" C.J. said, wrinkling his nose.

"Irish stew?" Mary said hopefully.

Jerry leaned over and looked into the kettle. "I'm
glad I emigrated."

"I thought if I put everything together and cooked it real slow," Mary said, "it would come out all hot and tasty."

"You are the love of my life, darlin'," Jerry said. "But I have to say it. You could cook that stuff till the millennium and it would get hot, but it don't look as though it'd ever get tasty."

Jake had slithered from Miranda's shoulders onto the bar and was creeping toward the kettle. She approached it, sniffed once, and quickly backed away. "You're no fool," Jack said as he fondled her ears.

"What have you got in there?" Bobby asked. "I see lumps."

"Beets," Mary answered. "And crumbled crackers—we still have a few boxes left—and the last of the bacon and some powdered milk and mustard and India relish and a couple of cans of beans. I think they were beans. The labels were gone off the cans."

"I'll try some, Mary," Miranda said stoutly. "I'm so hungry I could eat dirt."

In silence, they watched Mary ladle out a serving, tuck a spoon into the bowl, and pass it down the line. Miranda took a deep breath, forced the spoon into her mouth, chewed once, swallowed with a mighty effort... and burst into tears.

"I'm sorry, Mary," she sobbed. "I'm sorry, I tried but it's—it's—*terrible*." She tried to gulp back her tears, but that only made her cry all the harder. "I know I'm bein' a baby, but... Oh, Auntie, why does everything always go all *wrong*?"

Lucy came around the end of the bar and patted

Miranda on the back. Miranda began to hiccup. "There, there," Lucy soothed. "This doesn't sound like the girl who used to complain that nothing ever happened to her."

"Yeah, Red," said Bobby. "Remember, things can always get worse."

"Ah, my Ridiculous Child," C.J. said with a tolerant smile. "I keep forgetting how very young you are. In the series of earthquakes that has marked my life, these straitened circumstances are but a faint rumble. We shall persevere. 'Tis in the nature of the artist to do so."

"'Tis also in the nature of the artist to starve," Mary said dolefully. "And I just proved it."

"*Pfah!* As Roberto has just reminded us, things can always get worse."

"So?" said Lucy.

"So *live*," he bellowed. "Live your life as though the Grim Reaper were breathing down your dainty little neck. Carpe diem! Laugh, you silly woman. *Laugh*."

"Oh, Charlie," Dulcie said. "I do love you."

"And I, you, Pet." He looked down at her, and the color drained from his face. "Carpe diem," he whispered to himself.

She frowned up at him, a puzzled expression in her lovely eyes. "Do you feel all right?" she asked anxiously.

C.J. took her tiny hands in his, sank slowly to one knee, and lifted his eyes to hers. "Marry me," he said huskily.

"Charlie!" she said in a stunned voice.

"Right here, right now," he said. "Here, in this rat hole. With nothing to eat but slumgullion, and no hope of rescue. Before God and all of our friends. By all that's holy, if I'm to meet my maker, it will be with you at my side."

Miranda stared at them with her mouth open, tears drying forgotten on her cheeks. *Yes*, she thought fervently. *Oh, Dulcie, say yes.*

Dulcie looked around the room—The Widow was nowhere near—then leaned over and in a frightened voice said, "What about Mamma? She'll never agree."

C.J. got stiffly to his feet. "Hang the witch," he said crossly. "You're over eighteen and this is California—you can do what you want. If a captain of a ship can marry people, why not the proprietor of a— Wait, wait!" he said excitedly, and began to rummage through his pockets. He came up with a dog-eared little rectangle of pasteboard and waved it in her face. "Wilbur Josephus Packer," he said. "Justice of the Peace. *Now* will you marry me?"

Dulcie's blue eyes brimmed with tears. "Yes," she said. "Yes, yes, yes!"

C.J. yelled something inarticulate and swept Dulcie up into his arms, her tiny feet dangling inches above the floor. "Put me down, you savage," she said, giggling merrily.

He deposited her, and she looked up into his face and said, "On one condition."

"Name it."

220

Dulcie turned and held out her hand to Miranda. "Will Miss Nellie O'Grady be my maid of honor?"

"Oh, Dulcie! Of course, I will!"

"Wait a minute, Boss," said Jerry, shaking his head. "I don't want to be a dose of cold water here, but don't yez need a license to get hitched? One of my dearest memories, it is, goin' down to City Hall to get the license for me and me darlin' Mary."

"Is that a fact?" C.J. said smugly. "Seems to me that's one of the first things I did when we got to sunny California. It's right upstairs in my luggage, even as we speak."

"You've had it all along?" Dulcie whispered.

"I'm always prepared, My Love. For the best as well as the worst."

At that moment, Bobby poked Miranda in the ribs and whispered, "Pipe the snake." Miranda followed his eyes and saw Sully edge away from the bar and slip quietly to the other side of the room, where The Widow was, as usual, dozing in the most comfortable chair by the fire.

While the others hugged and squealed delightedly and babbled congratulations, Miranda and Bobby sat tensely on their bar stools and watched a pantomime play itself out across the room. Sully bent down and spoke into Bessie McGill's ear—she started to rise from her chair, her face purpling with rage.... Sully continued to talk, gesturing animatedly—she nodded; he helped her to her feet and smiled nastily in C.J.'s direction.... They began to walk toward the bar.

"It was nice while it lasted," Bobby said with a sigh. "Battle stations, Boss!" he called out.

The Widow stalked up to the bar, her footsteps echoing ominously in the silence that had fallen, and stopped in front of the happy couple.

"Dulcinea?" said The Widow.

Dulcie stared dumbly at her mother.

"You intend to marry this horrid little man?"

"I do," she said tremulously.

The Widow folded her arms. Her face was expressionless. "Then don't expect my blessing," she snapped, and stalked from the room.

"*Phew!*" said Miranda.

"I certainly expected her to say more than that," said Lucy.

"So did I," Dulcie said, frowning. "She's got something up her sleeve."

"It's like waiting for the world's biggest shoe to drop," Bobby remarked. "What do you suppose her next move's gonna be?"

"To Outer Mongolia, if I have my way," C.J. said, and glanced fondly at Dulcie, who was nestled against his shoulder. "Unless, Dearest, you insist she live with us after the nuptials?" he said sweetly.

Dulcie shuddered. "Don't even joke about it!"

Within minutes, preparations were under way. Miranda and Bobby and Jack went upstairs to strip the bedrooms of lace curtains to veil the bride and drape the dance-hall stage into the approximation of an altar. Lucy was downstairs practicing on the tuneless piano, and Mary was sweeping the floors, attempting to make a barren saloon at least look clean. This was going to be more than a mere wedding—this was going to be an American Moving Picture Company one-reeler!

Jerry had approached C.J. with the suggestion that, as precious little filmmaking was going on these days, there was plenty of unused stock and perhaps he would like a moving picture of the happy event? He had it all figured. Jack could crank the camera with a little rehearsal (as long as he kept the rhythm even and didn't get creative there was nothing to it, really) so Jerry could still be the best man, as C.J. had requested. "Genius!" was C.J.'s response. "A permanent nitrate record of the glorious day I took My Pet in glorious matrimony!"

Dulcie was coming out of the women's bedroom with the wardrobe wedding dress over one arm, humming "Ah, Sweet Mystery of Life" and practically skipping, when Miranda heard Sully whisper her name from the top of the stairs. Miranda motioned to Bobby and Jack, and they tiptoed to stand behind the open bedroom door.

"Oh, Dulcie," said Sully. "Why are you doing this?"

They heard Dulcie cry out. Miranda peeked cautiously around the edge of the door. "He grabbed her arm," she mouthed.

"Mr. Randall," Dulcie gasped. "Unhand me!"

"I'm gonna murder that guy," Bobby growled. He started to move forward, but Jack barred him with an arm across the chest. "Let her handle it," he whispered.

"I'm sorry, Dulcinea," he said, and they heard him sigh theatrically. "But you are the one who is hurting me. Why are you marrying that man?"

"Because," Dulcie said in a cold voice, "I happen to love him."

Miranda smiled and gave Bobby a thumbs-up.

"You deserve better than that bald-headed popinjay," Sully said petulantly. "Someone who can show you the finer things in life, someone with taste and breeding—"

"Like you, Mr. Randall?" Miranda peered through the crack where the door met the molding just in time to see Dulcie wrench her wrist out of his grasp. "I think your behavior shows a distinct lack of breeding," she said. "Now leave me alone. I have things to do." She backed away from him, turned, and sped down the stairs.

Sully stared after her for a minute, then stomped down the hall with an unbecoming scowl on his patrician features. "Just you wait," he muttered sullenly. "This isn't over, not by a long chalk. No one talks to Sullivan Carstairs Randall like that—" He went into the men's bedroom at the far end of the hall and slammed the door shut, cutting off his stream of injured invective.

"Well!" said Jack. "That explains why he and The Widow have been so thick. He's sweet on Miss McGill—"

"—and she thought she could snag Dulce a Boston Brahmin," Bobby finished.

Miranda laughed. "Not very smooth technique for a great lover."

Bobby grinned at her. "He ain't got a patch on The Boss, and that's a fact."

The afternoon sun was shining fitfully through the dust-smeared windows of The Lucky Greenback when Lucy seated herself at the battered upright and flexed her hands. C.J. nodded to Jack, who bent over Baby and began to crank. Lucy brought her hands down on the chipped keys for the opening notes of "Jesu, Joy of Man's Desiring." (If C.J. wanted the Wedding March from *Lohengrin*, he could play it himself on a comb and tissue paper, she had informed him in an uncharacteristic display of temper—but a very characteristic display of musicianship.)

C.J. stood on the little stage, shivering in a pinstripe suit (under which he wore long johns, two pairs of socks, and a flannel shirt) and cracking his knuckles. The Donnellys stood to one side, arm in arm, beaming sentimentally. Mary was already crying, tears trickling down her plump cheeks. The Widow and Sully stood by the front windows in stony silence.

"You're on, Red," Bobby said, and gave her a gentle push forward.

Why am I so jittery all of a sudden? Miranda wondered. *I haven't been scared of the camera since the very first time, back in the vacant lot on Pine Street. I feel like a hundred butterflies are fighting in my stomach.* She took a deep breath, folded her hands at her waist, and walked down the length of the room toward the altar, in time with the music. When she reached the end of the room and stepped up onto the stage to stand beside the Donnellys, C.J. stopped cracking his knuckles and gave her a wide smile. There were tears shining in his eyes.

Slowly, Zeb clomped down the stairs with Dulcie on his arm. She wore a simple, long-sleeved frock of white mull trimmed with tatting and had arranged a dusty net lace curtain over her flowing curls. In her trembling hands she held a grimy bouquet of beaded-wire daisies Miranda had found in the pantry. She looked ethereal, adorable, and exquisitely happy.

Zeb escorted her up onto the stage, then stumbled over to Bobby, who had quietly followed them up the aisle and taken his place opposite the Donnellys—out of the action but still within camera range. Zeb fumbled in his pockets, pulled out an enormous red bandanna, and lustily blew his nose. Dulcie handed her bouquet to Miranda and slipped her hand into C.J.'s, and they turned to face each other.

Wilbur Packer cleared his throat and opened his well-thumbed Bible. "Dearly beloved," he began, "we are gathered here in the sight of God and this company..."

This company, thought Miranda. *This wonderful company*. She had never been to a wedding before, and from articles and photographs in *The Ladies Home Journal* and *Collier's Magazine* had always envisioned them as grand affairs with bowers of smilax and orange blossoms, enough bridesmaids to populate the Ziegfeld *Follies*, booming organ music, a minister who looked like a Supreme Court justice, and all the guests in top hats or expensive gowns. But as she listened to Wilbur reciting the fine, simple words in his cracked old voice and gazed around at the faces of those she held most dear, she knew she would not have traded this makeshift ceremony in a freezing saloon in a ghost town in the Sierras for all the pomp and grandeur in the world.

". . . I now pronounce you man and wife," Wilbur said.

And the other shoe dropped.

The Widow marched across the room and onto the stage with Sully two steps behind, and yanked Dulcie's hand out of C.J.'s. "You've had your entertainment for the day," she said, "but it's over. You, Mister Turner, will keep your filthy hands off my daughter."

"We are married now," he said icily. "And there's nothing you can do—or *say*—about it."

The Widow smiled triumphantly, a tight drain hole of a smile that drew her mouth up like the strings of a purse. "It's not legal," she stated flatly. "Mr. Randall informs me that in the state of California, marriage requires a three-day wait, a blood test, and a license."

C.J.'s eyes found Jerry's. "Many's the time," he said evenly, "that you have kept me from killing the creature. What say you now, old friend?"

Jerry took a step forward and knotted his fists. "This toime I'll help ye, man." His brogue was very thick, a sure sign of strong emotion. "Me and Calhoun'll t'row her out in the snow. The wolves c'n have her. If they c'n stomach her."

"No, Charlie, no!" Dulcie wailed. "Not again—" She buried her face in her hands and began to weep.

Wilbur Packer began to laugh, cackling and snorting and slapping his bowed thighs until he was struggling for breath.

"You *annoying* little troll," The Widow barked at him. "Stop it!"

"Cain't, lady," he gasped. "I'm havin' too much fun. You ain't in Californy no more. Ain't been fer days."

"What?" C.J. and The Widow said in unison.

Dulcie lifted her face from her hands. "Whu-huh-hut?" she sobbed.

Wilbur slapped his thigh again. "Heh-heh-heh. I love this."

Miranda began to smile. *Two weeks with The Boss,* she thought, *and he's learned to milk the moment.*

"Ah, Sully," Wilbur sniggered. "Sully, Sully, Sully."

Sully's nostrils flared imperiously. "Are you addressing me?"

"You jest cain't rely on them old maps," Wilbur said with relish. "Cullersville sits dead smack on the border, and the Greenback here is in Nevaddy. And in Nevaddy—as any duckbrain knows—they ain't no wait and no need fer a license. What jest happened here is as legal as the Constitution of these Yew-nited States!"

He grinned at C.J. and shut his Bible with a slap. "You may kiss the bride."

And C.J. did.

"All's well that ends well," Miranda said, turning to Bobby with shining eyes.

The face that met hers was sober. "Check the calendar, Red."

Miranda's face sagged. "No," she whispered. "Not already—"

"Christmas Eve," he said, and bit his lip. "It's Christmas Eve."

Going Home

Lucy's bargain had run out, the last grains of sand sliding through the hourglass. California was over. Bobby and Jack and Zeb and all the pretty little horses, over. Letters would be written, impassioned with loss and do-you-remember, but the time between them would lengthen as they all moved on to other pursuits, other friends, other lives. Then cards at Christmas, then faded snapshots and bittersweet memories.

C.J. and Dulcie and the Donnellys, over. The brave dream that was The American Moving Picture Company, over. Playacting and dressing up and learning to be a real actress, the serious art that was so much fun, over. *I'm not even upset*, Miranda thought dully. *I'm just numb. Numb and sad.* "Now our revels are ended," she whispered.

The joyous celebration (joyous except for Sully and The Widow, who were nursing their wounds in a corner and plotting who knew what fruitless revenge) was suddenly unbearable. Miranda slipped from the room and fled to the kitchen.

Lucy was seated at the table, her head on her arms, sobbing as though the world had ended. Jake crouched at the other end of the table, immobile as a bookend, observing her placidly. Miranda stood in the doorway, unable to move. Lucy's gray eyes spilled over frequently, and she wept at sad songs and deathbed scenes in moving pictures, but this unfettered weeping was new, and Miranda was frightened.

The moment stretched on, Miranda sensing rather than hearing the boisterous clamor drifting in from the front room, the faint purring deep in Jake's chest. Finally, Lucy lifted her head. She stared at the girl, tears gliding over her swollen cheeks, her shoulders jerking convulsively.

Wordlessly, Miranda took a dish towel from the drainboard and handed it to her. Lucy wiped her face. "Weddings always make me cry," she said thickly.

Miranda sat beside her and reached out a hand. Lucy took it and they sat for a moment, then Miranda said, "What is it, Auntie?"

Lucy's mouth twisted. "I'm homesick."

Miranda turned her head away and looked out the window. *I've been so selfish*, she thought. *I never even thought about whether or not she was happy.*

"I'm sorry, darling," Lucy said. "Put it down to the strain of wondering if we're ever going to get out of this wretched hovel." She withdrew her hand and began pleating the damp towel into folds. "And then I remembered that it was Christmas Eve. Had you forgotten?"

Miranda shook her head.

"I had, until a few moments ago. And I started

thinking about being all warm and cozy in my kitchen—and the smells! I'd just about kill for the smell of a roast turkey, that wonderful rich smell when you open the door to baste it and the heat comes up into your face. I thought about all our friends coming in to trim the tree and sing carols and pretend they like eggnog. You remember, darling, the way we always did?" She stared blindly at her hands. "This is ridiculous."

The wind flung a fistful of sleet against the window, rattling the panes. Miranda shivered and blew on her hands, then tucked them in her sleeves. *A year ago tonight I was standing on an empty station platform,* she thought. *If nothing happens to me for the rest of my life, at least I'll have this year. I've seen the prairies and the desert and been chased by the Keystone Cops. I was in so many moving pictures I lost count. I rode horseback by the Pacific Ocean at sunset with a real cowboy. I saw The Birth of a Nation before the president did. I went to Babylon and made D. W. Griffith laugh. And The American was finally together again, the way I always wanted. I had my year. I can't ask for more.*

"We'll get out if we have to walk all the way down the mountain," Miranda said with a trace of her old fire. "Then . . . we'll go home."

"That's my girl," Lucy said, laughing shakily. "That's my never-give-up girl."

"I'm sorry, Auntie, truly I am. Nothing's worked out, has it? It's all my fault. I never should have dragged you into this."

Lucy laughed again, this time with genuine amusement. "Do you honestly think I live my life by the whims of a thirteen-year-old girl? You didn't drag me into anything I didn't want to be dragged— Let me rephrase that. Yes, we certainly got off to a rocky start, and no, nothing has gone according to plan. But it was *my* decision to come here, not yours."

"And now you're homesick," Miranda said wistfully.

"Of course I'm homesick. Aren't you?"

"No."

"I like that," Lucy said indignantly. She blew her nose on the towel and smoothed away the last traces of tears. "I break my back to make a home for us, and you don't even have the grace to appreciate it. Well, I miss it even if you don't. I miss my students, such as they are, and my garden, and funny old Mrs. Norwood, and—"

Miranda's mouth went dry. "You're not talking about New Jersey," she whispered hoarsely. "Are you?"

"New Jersey!" Lucy repressed a shudder. "I never knew what a stuffy old horror Leewood Heights was till I got shed of the place. A pox on New Jersey!"

Miranda threw her hands in the air. "I give up! Here I've been—" She glared at Lucy. "Good night, Irene! I've been going around all year with a knot in my stomach the size of—of—*Texas* thinking because you and C.J. made that darned bargain I better enjoy the hell out of each day— Oh, I quit!"

"You'd better quit that language, Missy, or I'll put you on the train myself! Wait just a minute—you knew about the pact?" She spread her hands. "That Gilmer boy's got a mouth like a swinging door."

Miranda stared at her, too stunned to say anything.

Lucy shook her head wonderingly. "I don't know. I just don't know what goes on in your head. Miranda?

Miranda, darling, look at me. Why didn't you just come to me and ask?"

"Afraid of the answer," Miranda replied.

"That's honest, at least. Did you really think I was going to pack up sticks the minute we got back to town? By the time we finish shooting the picture, why that's another month at least." She chuckled to herself. "Or two, if that man doesn't quit changing the plot every time the wind shifts. You could've saved your long face for Valentine's Day!"

"Yes, ma'am." Miranda giggled and said, "Now I've done it. Anytime I do something you don't like, it'll be 'Back to New Jersey with you, young lady!'"

"Thank you, Miranda Louise." Lucy smiled. "You have just given me the ammunition I need to keep you in line for years."

"Fine." Miranda smiled back at her. "As long as we're sharing secrets, what about Zeb?"

Lucy's eyes dropped to the table, and she began fidgeting with the towel again. "I don't know what you mean. . . . Oh, I guess I do." She lifted her eyes to Miranda's. "I think he's as nice a fellow as you'd ever want to meet."

"Nice? He's in *love* with you, for crying out loud."

"Don't push me, honey. I know he's not fancy—"

"Pooh!" Miranda snorted. "C.J.'s plenty fancy, and look where it's gotten us. Halfway up a mountain with nothing to eat but crackers and snow. I like Zeb, Auntie, I always did. Are you going to marry him?"

"Merciful heavens!" Lucy blushed, her cheeks turning a bright pink. "He hasn't even asked me."

"He will," Miranda said serenely. "Just as soon as

he screws up the courage, which I'm guessing will be sometime around 1934." She leaned back in her chair and stretched luxuriously, flinging her arms wide. "Farewell, New Jersey! Hollywood, here I come!

"With one addition," she said after a moment.

Again, Lucy blushed. "I told you, I'm not getting married."

"Actually," Miranda said carefully, "I was referring to Jake. I'm keepin' her."

Jake lifted her head.

"See?" said Miranda. "She knows we're talking about her."

Jake's tail began to switch back and forth. Her head was cocked at an angle, her ears laid flat against her head.

"Look at her," Lucy said disgustedly. "I swear that thing's possessed."

Jake whined low in her throat and jumped from the table. She paused, glanced back at Miranda, and trotted purposefully from the room.

Miranda jumped up. "She wants us to follow her!"

"Really, Miranda."

"Come *on*."

Jake trotted down the hall to the main room, Miranda following anxiously, Lucy indulgently. The wedding party was gathered around the fireplace, halfway through a giddy rendition of "The Daring Young Man on the Flying Trapeze." C.J. spotted Lucy and bellowed, "Terpsichore, come play for us!"

Jake went to the front window, bounded up onto the sill, and began to howl.

"What is it, Miss Lucy?" Jack called out.

"I don't know," she said. "That blasted cat again."

Jake was pawing the window. Miranda picked her up, and she twisted in the girl's arms, meowing insistently. Miranda rubbed the frost away with her sleeve and peered out the window. "Hush up!" she cried. "She hears something—*hush up!*"

Bobby unfolded himself from the floor with a groan. "Oh brother, what now?"

"*Hush!*" Miranda screamed. "Oh, *you*—" She ran to the door with Jake in her arms and yanked it open savagely. The wind whirled in to an angry chorus of "Shut the door!" Jack and Bobby crossed the room quickly and followed Lucy onto the porch.

Miranda was standing at the far end of the porch, staring down the hill. "Listen," she said urgently. "*Listen.*"

"Listen to what?" Bobby said. "I don't hear—Wait! You're right, Red. Something's out there."

The sound was faint, at first no more than a cry on the wind, then growing louder as it lifted up and the echo caromed off the mountains. A high, thin, reedy wail...

Miranda adjusted her hold on Jake and pointed with a shaking finger. Far away, in the valley below, was a fat puff of smoke. Then another, and another.

"By gum!" Jack exclaimed. "It's a train!"

"Jake heard it," said Miranda. "She heard the whistle."

"I guess Mr. Ince got our message after all," said Jack with a grin. "Looks like he sent the posse."

"In the fine old tradition of every two-bit two-reeler," Bobby cracked. "Hey, Jack, let's go tell The

Boss we got the finale. Hope Jer' didn't waste all the stock on the nuptials." His eyes briefly locked on Miranda's, and she jerked her head toward Lucy and nodded brightly.

Bobby's eyes widened. "Miss Lucy?" he said diffidently.

She turned her head. "Yes, Robert?"

"You—you aren't going back East?"

"No," she said, smiling gently at him. The relief flooding his face was poignant. "No, Bobby dear, we're not. You'll always have a home with us, for as long as you want."

"Thank you, Miss Lucy," he said slowly. "This year with you and Miranda's been . . . the only real home I've ever known. And the best—" He broke off, and Miranda watched him fight his emotions in the seconds it took for him to arrange his features into their habitual cocksure mask. "Then you're stuck with me," he said lightly.

He said it, Miranda thought. *He finally said it*.

"Come on, cowboy," Bobby said to Jack. "Let's go spread the good word."

They made for the door and burst through together, dramatically shouting: "We're saved! Help is on the way!"

Miranda stood with her nose buried in Jake's golden ruff, quivering with a hundred different emotions as she listened to the screams and joyous shouts inside the old saloon. The smoke was clearly visible now, streaming behind the engine as it chugged up the narrow switchbacks, the cowcatcher sending up great glittering spumes of snow as the valiant little train breasted the drifts that choked the rails. The whistle sounded again, sharp and fierce in the frosty air.

They had a few seconds before the Company came flooding out onto the porch, a fleeting chance to savor the moment. Lucy put her arms around Miranda and they gazed silently at the mountains rising against the winter sky, washed in vibrant shades of purple and gold and orange by the setting sun.

"Merry Christmas, darling girl."

"We're going home, Auntie. We're going home."

Coming soon!

Miranda Goes to War

Turn the page for a sneak preview of
the further adventures of Miranda Gaines
and The American Moving Picture Company. . . .